MW01516251

The Trail of the Wolf

BRUCE BRILLIANTINE

NEWMAN SPRINGS PUBLISHING
320 Broad Street
Red Bank, NJ 07701

First originally published by Newman Springs Publishing 2022

ISBN 978-1-64801-427-7 (Paperback)
ISBN 978-1-64801-428-4 (Hardcover)
ISBN 978-1-64801-429-1 (Digital)

Printed in the United States of America

To all who may or may not have beasts in their lives, I hope you enjoy and relate to the narrative.

Preface

Hello and welcome. My name is Bruce, and you will be accompanying me on a journey. We will be traveling with Dr. Jordan Blaine who has run into an evil beyond his wildest imagination. He is frightened for himself, his family, and the rest of humanity. Dr. Blaine feels compelled to stop this deadly killer which is more beast than human, and, as always, a few steps ahead of the doctor and the authorities. Yet the beast leaves a blatant trail of blood, mutilation, and death.

Easy to follow, if you dare, but very difficult to figure out where the trail leads and how to stop the beast before he takes his next victim.

As men, we have some idea of good and evil. Good is something we desire and move toward. It gives our life hope and an emotional and spiritual strength in our life. While evil is destructive, painful. It destroys our very soul, separates us from things we love, and eventually shortens our lives. But what happens when you discover an evil that is so horrific and so terrible that it's very existence demands that you confront it and destroy it?

As Dr. Blaine pursues the beast, he discovers that he is being led and often manipulated, ending up further away from people he loves and the life he has known. But isn't this what beasts do? They change your life for the worse, giving you no rest. They lead you through their trail of death, horror, and destruction. Yet the pursuit offers a sense of fulfillment, of accomplishment as you get closer and closer to destroying your beast. That is, until you look back upon your own trail.

Dr. Blaine hasn't looked back; he is still hot on the pursuit of this crafty killer. At some point, he will have to look back and see what he's gone through because then he will have an idea of the direction in which he is headed.

Travel with Dr. Jordan Blaine as he tries to access who and what this killer is and why it is bent on so much death and destruction.

It was a nice ten days visiting relatives in Michigan. We would be home in a day and a half of driving. My wife was particularly happy to have seen her parents since it's been nearly three years since the last visit. Luckily here, I'm on sabbatical this year and have some extra time for studying abroad. Our two girls, twenty and twenty-two, in the backseat were also thrilled to go on a road trip, although they acted more like eight and ten once the trip started, pushing and shoving each other, with one especially complaining to get one-upmanship on the other. You'll get, "She is it hitting me." The other one would retort, "Well, you hit me first." They acted just like they were kids again. I didn't say anything because I was remembering a time in the past when they were young and cute and easy to control.

Having gotten a late start, we were only six hours into the trip home and it was nearly ten o'clock at night. I thought I would push for another hour before we got a motel. Goodbyes seem to take such a long time, and maybe that I'm in my fifties, it doesn't seem so important to get the 6:00 a.m. start in the morning to make time. I just kind of let things happen and move with the flow, and if we don't leave real early, it's okay. We will still get home tomorrow, just a little later. Right now, the girls are playing with their electronic devices—MP3s, iPhones, Kindle fires—whatever instrument they choose for the moment. My wife, on the other hand, is raving about how wonderful it was to go home and see her parents; how they and the home they lived in had not changed one bit in the past three years. She was recounting all the visits and memories of visits that we had previously made. I, on the other hand, am trying to keep my eyes on the road with an ear to her conversation. She has been about three hours on this present subject. When she's excited and on a roll, I'm not going to rain on her parade. So every now and then, I interjected a few supportive words like "that was fun" and "we'll make sure we do that next time."

I'm not rushed for time too much these days. I'm on sabbatical for the next six months and plan to take a few courses overseas. I'm a medical doctor, and I teach anatomy and physiology at a medical school. The subject matter hasn't changed very much in the past five or 6,000 years, but it's the technology that's hard to keep up with and I thought I'd take another course on magnetic resonance imaging. Occasionally, we will do an autopsy for the state police, but most of the time is spent in the lab dissecting cadavers with future doctors. I, in particular, find this work extremely rewarding and fascinating. Anatomy is taught in the first year of medical school, and all the young doctors are so enthusiastic and bright-eyed, and I still have some extra time to speak to them on the subject. They very much enjoy learning about disease processes, and then get a chance to view the degenerative disease processes on the bodies we are dissecting.

Sometimes I'll have a few of them—the brighter students— help me with the state police autopsies. These are usually murder cases that have to be carefully examined and evaluated as to the cause of death and the type of injuries sustained. Even though I love my work, it will be nice not having to see a dead person in the next six months.

We've taken a shortcut; one that we have taken before. It saves us about twenty miles and keeps us from getting caught in a *lot* of city traffic. It's a backwoods highway with no streetlights and sparsely populated—a nice quiet drive. Wait a minute. There's something in the highway. It's a little girl, six or eight years of age, and she is standing in the path of our car and waving for us to stop. I had to quickly put on the brakes because she came running out of the woods right in front of our car. My wife grabs me by the arm and says, "Be careful, Jordan. You don't know who else is around."

I am concerned. There is a young child with blood on her left shoulder running to my driver's door. She's hysterical. She's screaming at me and pounding on my window, "Please, help me! Please! He's killing my family! Please help them!"

My wife looks at me and says, "We need to call the authorities."

I look at her and say, "You need to call the authorities. These people need help now." I open the door and reach under my seat for the pistol that I keep there, loaded in a case of an emergency. I have a permit which was easy to get since I work with the state police. The little girl is pulling on my arm. I look at her bleeding shoulder and I ask, "Are you all right?"

She wasn't concerned about herself. She just pulled on my shoulder and said, "Please come."

I looked more closely at her shoulder and saw something like claw marks which went from the top of her shoulder, about nine inches down her back left side. There were four claw marks; each was about three inches apart. I thought to myself, *What could have done that?*

She started pulling on my hand even before I closed the car door. I asked her what happened, and she said a big hairy man had broken the front door down and came in and attacked her family while they were sitting at the dinner table. Her father got up and started to stop him, and the hairy man bit him on the neck. Her mother picked up a bread knife and started stabbing the bad man and yelled for her to run to get help. As she was running out the door to go to the highway to get help, the bad man tried to grab her by the shoulder. She managed to escape and ran to the road for help.

The little girl started running ahead of me. She went down dirt driveway, and I could see lights from a home about 200 yards down the path. I ran along and caught up with her. I didn't want her going in by herself. There was a sense of urgency in both of us. Hers was to save the lives of her family as she ran without fear and without caution. My sense of urgency was more reserved because I had no idea what was waiting for me as I approached the cabin. I knew I wanted to help these people, but I also knew I had to protect this little girl and my family.

It was a large log cabin-style house, three or four bedrooms and a large front porch. When we got within twenty-five feet of the porch, I could see that the doors; they were pushed in—one was hanging only by the bottom hinge, otherwise it would be flat on the floor. The other door was flat on the floor about five feet into the home. I asked the girl her name, and she said it was June. I told her to sit on the porch and watch for the police. I didn't want her going inside. I didn't want to go inside but there are some things you just have to do.

I didn't have to go through the doorway very far to see her parents or what were pieces of them. I asked June how many other people were in the house. She said her mother, father, and older sister. I looked back in, and there was an arm here, intestinal contents there, blood splattered all over the floor walls and ceiling. There was the smell of fresh blood. I glanced at a man's torso lined up against the wall. I could see bite marks on the neck and that he was missing an arm but the rest of the body was completely drenched in blood, with claw marks all over his torso shredding his garments and flesh. The mother's body was on the other side of the room. She had only one

11

noticeable injury and that was a clawing blow to the right side of her neck which almost decapitated her. It looks like the girl's father had put up one courageous fight, having sustained most of the injuries. I can see all the furniture in the room broken or thrown about.

Everything was blood spattered—the walls, tables, and ceiling showed where blood had spurted out. There were parts of the wall six or seven feet above the floor where it looks like his body was dragged, leaving a smear of blood. There were pieces of flesh literally stuck and dripping blood from the wall as if they had been ripped off and thrown with great force. And now I'm thinking, *Why am I being so analytical in my observing such a horrific scene?* Is it my medical training or just my way of distancing myself from such a horrific scene where this poor kid's family was just butchered while they were still alive?

It was hard stepping into the room without getting some blood or tissue on your feet. I was concerned about her older sister of whom I had seen no trace of. I started to search the other rooms and closets; maybe she was hiding. I was also worried about June because I didn't want her to come inside. I yelled out to June, "Keep watching for the police! Don't come in!" I think she knew at some level that it was better for her to stay outside on the porch. Well, anyway, I had to keep searching. I started yelling, "Hello! Hello! Is anybody there?" I thought I should have asked June her sister's name. And then it didn't matter. I saw her or what was left of her. She was lying on the floor of the second bedroom that I searched. There she was lying alone in a pool of blood. The bed was made, the curtains were drawn—nothing was out of place in the room, except for the fact it was a young girl on the floor with her back and legs shredded down to the bone. There was no blood or tissue thrown anywhere else in the room. Where was the rest of her?

Then I remembered from many years ago when I was a hunter and had seen partially devoured animals. He had eaten her.

I went back out onto the porch with June. I noticed that I was tracking blood onto the porch. But I also noticed that there were tracks of blood where I had not walked. They were fresh, wide paw marks, about seven inches long and nine inches wide. They were very canine-looking, with three pads attached with clawed toes. These animallike tracks ran down the porch and into the woods. They appear to belong to a bipedal animal with a stride of about seven feet. I wanted to see if it left any tracks in the dirt where it left the porch but I needed a flashlight to check that out. I thought I would tell the police about the tracks. I grabbed June by the hand, and we started walking back to my car.

A police car with lights flashing suddenly appeared to be coming down the driveway. I put my pistol in my back pocket and brought June to the police car. It was an older police car, six or eight years old; something that would be used by a small department in a backwater town. The police officer, who happened to be the chief, got out of the car and immediately tried to take control by asking what the problem was and who was injured. I introduced myself and told the officer what happened and what I had found. I said that it was my wife who called in the report while I went to investigate. I suggested that he call an ambulance for June for her injuries and that she wait in the car while I show him the cabin. I also suggested that he may want to take a flashlight because there might be some interesting tracks he might want to see.

The chief grabbed his microphone out of the car and called in for an ambulance and state police backup for a homicide. He took June and placed her in the car and told her he would be right back and for her to wait there quietly while we checked out the scene.

We walked to the cabin in a fast walk the, and he mumbled something about having to secure the scene. I told him that I was a medical doctor and that I do autopsies for the state police and that this was one of the most horrific things I had ever seen. And he said "Okay, okay" like I was an amateur. Well, when we got to the door, he looked inside. He stopped and didn't move. He just looked about the room. The more he looked the more his jaw dropped open. Then he backed out the doorway, saying, "What could have done this?" He was looking really pale and shaken. I told him about the two bodies in the living room and the body of the daughter in the bedroom. I assured him that they were deceased, dead, and that I was a medical doctor who could diagnose such things. He then said there was probably no need for him to go in, wanting to keep the integrity of the crime scene intact. I then directed him to the tracks leading off the porch. At this point, I was probably leading him on the investigation, but I wanted to see if there were any footprints in the soil coming from the porch. And there they were, leading off the porch into the woods a distance of about fifteen yards.

There wasn't much vegetation around the house. The owners had probably sprayed weedkiller to keep vegetation down in case of a fire. In the distance, we could hear the state police cars coming. The chief said, "The state police are here. This is a job for them."

We hurried back to his car to check on June. I told the chief that I wanted to check on my wife and two daughters in the car on the road and he nodded okay and I hurried down the driveway. As I reached the end of the driveway, the ambulance was pulling up, and I pointed them down to the police car. I hurried across the road to my wife and daughters to see how they were doing and put the pistol back under my front seat. I figured that if they didn't see the pistol, they wouldn't have to check it out.

My wife was all questions about what happened and if everybody is okay and if anybody is injured. I wave my hand to her to be quiet and slowly said, "It's very bad."

My daughters chimed in, "What do you mean, Dad, by very bad?"

I said, "They had been torn apart."

The look on all three of their faces was that of shock and surprise. Then my wife said, "There was nothing you could do for any of them."

I just said, "No."

My oldest daughter asked, "Was the person who did it still there?"

I said, "He had left. There were tracks leading off the porch and into the woods."

Just about this time, a state trooper car was coming our way, screaming down the road with its siren on. I call the family to sit tight and directed the car down to the chief and the ambulance. I went down to see what was happening, not that I thought I was going to be needed that much but I was interested in how the investigation was going to proceed.

The ambulance crew had already bandaged June's shoulder and she was sitting in the back of the ambulance on a stretcher. Her eyes followed me as I walked by. I wanted to grab her and hold her, and tell her everything was going to be all right, but I knew it wasn't. I hurried up to be with the trooper and the chief and asked if I could come along. The trooper looked back at me like I was a civilian who shouldn't be delving into police business. The chief said that I was a doctor and the person that found the victims. The trooper said, "Just stay behind us and don't touch anything." We walked up to the door, and the trooper peered inside. He immediately started to give orders to the chief, "I want this whole area cordoned off. I don't want anyone else to see this. Keep everyone away." He looked at me and said, "No talking to anyone about what you've seen. We will need a statement from you before you go." Then he said to the chief, "There's a special unit that handles this type of thing. I have to give them a call." Then he left to go back to his patrol car.

Since it looks like I would be there for some time before they would take a statement, I told the chief I was going to send my family to a motel we had passed a few miles back. When I got back to my car, the kids were asleep and my wife was impatiently waiting to get back on the road. She was a little aggravated to find out that they would have to stay at a motel for the night. I said that this was part of the police procedure and that since we had gotten involved in this, now we had to see it through.

It wasn't too long that the special unit arrived. They drove up in black Suburbans with black suits, and they immediately took charge. Their main spokesman arranged for the ambulance to take June to a special hospital for evaluation. He had the chief and the trooper remove their cars to the road and asked them to do traffic and crowd control. While he was ordering the locals around, the rest of his group started sealing off the cabin from about twenty yards out. The others started taking pictures of the cabin and the front doorway. They were well coordinated. They look like they had done this before. The main man told me I had to stick around for debriefing. He said I cannot talk to anyone about what happened, including the police. It seemed that this new group had taken over the whole investigation and that the local police were on a need to know status. Since it was late and would be a while, I asked the chief if I could rest in the front seat of his car. He said, "Sure."

About an hour later, several other Suburbans showed up, the occupants flashed their badges and drove into the crime scene. I got out of the car to see what was happening. It appeared that the main man's superior had just arrived. Now they started bringing out flood lamps and generators and more men who were combing onto the grounds. They were taking more pictures and doing more measurements and taking blood samples. They took samples of blood on the deck, on the door, off the walls, and of bite marks on the victims. Some of these, I am sure, were trying to get DNA samples of the killer. They measured footprints, they measured bite mark, they took pictures of measuring bite marks, and they took pictures of all the injuries. They even took my picture. These men were very thorough in processing the complete crime scene.

It was finally my time to talk to the director of this investigation. He introduced himself as John Gilleland. He said he would be taking my statement and asked me to describe everything that had happened, trying not to leave out any detail going from the beginning to right now. As he was listening, I noticed he was taping me. I didn't mind because I often tape conversations during autopsies. I told him everything I could with every detail I could think of. It took me about half an hour to describe my part of what happened. He told me not to talk to anyone about what had happened and that I could leave. He also said that this was a federal investigation now and that the penalties for discussing this with anyone else but him were severe. I was curious and tried to start up a conversation with the man. I asked him what department of the government employed him. He said he worked with the Center for Disease Control out of Atlanta, Georgia. Since I had worked with many people at the CDC, I dropped a few names to him. He said he didn't work in their department.

Continuing from right now, he asked me to step into his Suburban. There was a desk with chairs, TV screens, computers, and communication consoles. It was a command center. On one wall, there were about fifteen rifles and shotguns lined up right and secured. There was a lot of storage area, boxes, camera equipment, Geiger counter, test tubes, and sample collection equipment which I recognized from the state police investigation that I had taken part in.

Continuing from before, he said that he didn't work in any department with which I would be familiar. I could believe that because most people at the CDC don't run around with rifles and shotguns. I also noticed he had a holster with a pistol in his suit jacket. I said to him I didn't believe the CDC was that much into law enforcement, motioning to the guns against the wall. He said, "Much depends upon the disease and the specific carrier." I tried to get a little more involved in the investigation and asked what he thought about the large caninelike footprints leading from the cabin. He said that he had seen them and that they didn't mean anything until he had completed a full investigation. He added, "They could have been from an animal that just stumbled onto the scene." I remarked that I've been hunting for over twenty-five years and I've never seen anything like these footprints. Trying to end the conversation as he walked out of the office, he said, "We won't know much until we do a computer match of all known animal footprints." Trying to keep up with him, I asked if I could ask one more question, and he said, "Yes." I said, "Those footprints which led off the porch into the woods, are you going to try to track them with trail dogs or anything?"

He said, "Yes, the dogs are due here between eight-thirty and nine tomorrow morning." That is when we will start tracking it.

I said, "Can I come along?"

He looked back at me and said, "Are you sure you know how to handle a shotgun?"

I said very emphatically, "Yes."

He said, "Sure. Be here at eight-thirty."

I called a cab to get me to my family's motel. I gave him instructions to pick me up at 8:00 a.m. Luckily, I had packed hiking boots and brush pants for the hunt. It was going to be only three or four hours sleep before I had to get up. My wife didn't approve of me getting this involved in the murders, but I told her this was something I thought I had to see through. I also told her I thought it would be a good idea if she drove the rest of the way home. I would try to fly back in the next couple of days.

Seven-thirty came too quickly but I still jumped out of bed, ready to go like a young man. The cab was waiting at 8:00 a.m. I got there a little before 8:30 to meet the rest of the posse. There were four or five more black Suburbans parked around the cabin, with a lot more men in black suits running around, gathering equipment. I was most interested in the dogs they were to use. There were four hound dogs and one police dog. The handlers for the hound dogs look like hunters I used to go coon hunting with; they were right off the farm. The handler for the police dog looks like a typical police K9 handler. He looked very out of place for this mission.

About 8:40 a.m., John Gilleland waved me over and told me we were going to start. He handled me a pump shotgun and told me it was loaded with the ammunition that I would need. He also told me to stay close to him and not go off on my own. He said, "We need to let the dogs do their job and stay behind them so they can follow the scent." I knew that, but I let him be the boss and instruct everybody on how this was to go.

When the dogs were taken over to where the tracks were coming off the porch, they all of a sudden got really quiet. They meandered around in a circle, whining and making little yelps like they were not happy to be there. Their handlers got them moving by saying things like "Come on, get them, boy!" Get in there!" "Herk in there. Herk 'em."

I asked John, "Have they been on this trail before?" And he just said, "Yes." We all got into a group behind the hounds as they took off into the woods, with the police dog following. The handlers were running behind them with long leashes. We were spread out about twenty yards wide in back of them. There were about fifteen men in black suits, myself, and four state troopers. We were all armed.

There were men carrying high-powered rifles, shotguns, AR-15s, and one look like he had a double barrel, a nitro express, an elephant gun. John had what looked like a .308 rifle with a twenty-shot clip. I think we were ready for almost anything.

We've gone about fifty yards into the woods, and I just had to take one of the shells out of my shotgun to see if it was buckshot or slugs. The shell read 00 buckshot, nine pellets. These were pretty standard defensive loads. What was unusual was that the shells look like they had been reloaded. I wasn't too worried, though, because I had ten men on either side of me who were very well armed.

All of a sudden, the dogs slowed down. They had hit a briar patch. The hounds and their handlers started to pick their way through it. The police dog's handlers started looking for a way around. Four of the men in suits started taking hair samples off of the briars, along with what look like DNA swabs of blood. These fellows were very thorough in their investigation. John ordered two of his other men to stand guard while they were taking samples. The rest of us went around to pick up the dogs on the other side of the briar patch.

After the briar patch, the dogs took off very quickly. The trees and brush were sparse, and they moved at a running pace. About a mile later, I noticed that the tone of the dogs' barking had changed. Having been a coon hunter for many years, I was trained to notice a difference in the dogs' bark when they finally treed the coon. This is how the hounds were now barking. When we got to where, they were barking up a tree and clawing at it as if it were trying to get up on it. The police dog was sitting up, also barking. This was a fifty- or sixty-foot tree about three feet wide. The handlers said, "Check up in the tree. We might have him treed."

We all started looking up at the tree, some of them with their rifles raised in an upward position like they were going to shoot something out of the tree. In order to see the top of the tree, we all had to back further away from the tree to see the top branches. So here we were, twenty men fifteen yards out, encircling a tree and looking for something. Eventually, the handlers decided that they should circle around the general area to see if they could take up the trail again. That was a wise move. Sometimes a treed coon will jump from tree to tree for fifteen or twenty yards, and then climbed down and take off again. A smart dog will circle around and pick up the trail if the coon isn't found in the tree with the scent.

Well, it was taking some time for the dogs to circle around the around the tree in widening circles. Everyone was sitting down, taking a break, and waiting for the trail to be picked up. I saw little dale or hollow about fifty yards away and thought I go down to take a peek and see what was down there. The brush was sparse and I noticed a clearing about ten more yards away. I went to take a look. I knew John told me to stay close by, but this was a chance for me to try out my wilderness expertise.

On coming up to the clearing, I stopped behind a bush just before the grass started. If you are a hunter or prey, you do not rush out into a clear area where you can be seen before you check it out. So I hunkered down behind the bush and peered out right and left to see if there was anything in the clearing which was about fifteen yards across. I didn't see anything and was just getting ready to stand up when I looked down where my feet were. Then I saw them—the tracks.

Those same large canine tracks. There were a few of them in one spot, like he had paused at the edge of the clearing a while before going across. I thought he knows what he's doing and I better check out the area a little better.

It looked like he went straight across the clearing. I thought maybe I should follow it but then I got this very uneasy feeling. The forest was very dense on the other side and he could be in there watching me, and in the clearing, I would be unprotected, except for this shotgun. Anything or anyone could be right over there in that dense foliage directly across from me in those... Wait a minute! There's something there. Behind one of the pines there was a large dark shape about six or eight feet tall. No, that couldn't be anything. My eyes are playing tricks? No, there is something there. I can see its eyes.

From my estimation, the body was about four and a half feet wide. The head was about three feet wide and full of hair. I lifted my glasses to focus a little better. My God, it moved. It was facing me and looking at me. It looked like it was grabbing an upper branch of the tree to support itself while it was watching me. It wasn't a bear. It moved more like a man. But it was as big as a bear. And one thing I knew, a shotgun would not stop a charging bear.

I slowly eased my safety off. I thought, *Whatever you do, don't start running.* It might initiate a predator pursuit. I just started slowly stepping backward—one, two, three steps—and he's still there. Ten steps and I'm still looking at him. Suddenly, I could hear the dogs picking up the trail again. They were coming my way. Then I took one last look at the looming figure and I turned and started to run. I called to the handlers and told them where he had rested where I saw him last. Then I told John what happened. He told me to stay with him and signaled his men to go on and investigate what I had seen. Of course, the men in suits rushed over, started investigating, and started taking samples where he paused before the clearing and where he stood behind the tree. The men were already at the position by the fir tree where he was resting and looking at me. It was interesting. When I arrived, I found that I couldn't reach the branch where I saw him rest his hand above his head. It was almost nine feet above the ground. He was bigger than I had thought.

The hounds took off again, followed by their handlers and the rest of us. They were moving fast in a straight line. Before the trail was more circuitous, twisting right and left like he was trying to throw us off his trail. Now it was more straight, like he was trying to quickly get away from us or get to some unknown destination fast. After a quick couple of miles, the trail led to a road. When we got to the other side of the road, the dogs were there, meandering around in a circle. They had lost the trail. The only thing on that side of the road was some car tracks where it looks like a SUV had been parked. John quickly got everyone away from that particular area in order to preserve the tire tracks. He told the dogs' handlers to circle around fifteen or twenty yards out in every direction to see if they can pick up the trail. Without any urging, the men in suits started taking pictures and measurements of the car tracks. John got out his cell phone and ordered the mobile laboratory to come to the site, as well as transportation for the rest of us.

After about half an hour, the dogs and their handlers came back and rested near the site. They had not picked up any trail. I asked John if this had this happen before. He said, "Yes." I casually made the statement, "It looks like he got in a vehicle and drove off."

John, being as definitive as he usually is, said, "It does appear that way, but he could have been picked up by another vehicle or run down the road, and for some reason, the dogs can't pick up the scent. We will have to check the whole area out for tracks and signs of other people being involved."

In about fifteen minutes, the command vehicle with the mobile lab and four other black Suburbans arrived. They started making plaster casts of the tire tracks and any other tracks they could find. They walked down the road both ways for a mile or two, looking out for any signs of someone recently being dropped off, walking on the shoulder, or anything else they deemed suspicious. They came up with nothing. John asked me to leave the shotgun at command center so it can be stored away. He and two other men were working with the computer to find out exactly what kind of vehicle left those tire tracks. It seems that if you match the type of tire with the measurements of the spacing between the tires, there is a computer program to tell you the type of vehicle you're looking for. This one turned out to be an American-made SUV, a Blazer.

I was there when they notified the state police to stop all SUVs of that make and model. They did know the color but they had to start somewhere. John asked me if I wanted a ride back to town, but I said, "If you don't mind me sticking around, I'm kind of enjoying watching you work this case."

I didn't expect him to say yes when he said, "Sure. We're sending out for lunch. Ham and cheese okay for you?"

I said "Yes." I thought maybe he's taking time to show off how good his operation is to a fellow professional. But later I found out he just wanted keep an eye on me.

The investigators were very busy. They did just about everything they did at the cabin site, including checking the dirt for hair fibers. A couple of hours had elapsed. We had had lunch, and they were starting to pack up to leave. One of the troopers ran over to John and told him that someone had been killed at a movie theater in a town about eight miles away. After hearing the preliminary report, he thought we should all take a look right away. John takes out a whistle and blows it. Everyone instantly stopped and paid attention. John said, "We might have another crime scene to investigate and we have to move now." I never saw people move so fast. Within two or three minutes, we were screaming down the highway with our sirens on. I was in the command vehicle with John. He was patched in on the phone to the local police. After a few questions about the crime scene, he was telling them to keep everyone away and that we would be there in fifteen minutes.

When we arrived near the town, we were at a top of a hill looking down into a valley. Cassville was a town of about 5,000 to 8,000 people. The movie theater was located at the edge of town surrounded by a large parking lot. We could see squad cars with flashing lights parked around the entrance to the theater. *Driving* closer to the theater, we could see three local squad cars and a state trooper car. They had already set up police lines and were doing crowd control. The state trooper, who seems to be in charge of the deployment, quickly came over to our Suburban and started giving John details of the crime scene. Initially, the most alarming thing I saw was one of the local police outside the theater on his knees, crying and throwing up while trying to hold himself up against one of the outside walls. Two other local police were keeping people outside the police lines. One was inside with several movie attendants directing customers away from the lobby and to the outside doors. The local police chief was in the middle of the lobby waiting for us.

As we walked up *to* the chief, he came forward, introduced himself, shook John's hand, and told John that he was glad to see him because this was way beyond anything he was used to seeing. He walked us over to the front of the ladies' restroom. There was a middle-aged female lying in front of the restroom door. Half of her face had been clawed off. She was deceased and probably died instantly because there was no sign of movement with the blood flow. The chief said that this wasn't the bad one. He pointed us to the inside of the restroom and just stood at the entrance. We could see why. It looked like someone had spray painted the walls with blood and guts. I had never seen so much blood and tissue-splattered walls, ceiling, and floor. As John and I stepped in, we saw what appeared to be the body of a young female lying face down. Her back had been raked down to the bone, but that wasn't the worst part. Something had ripped open her chest and intestines and slung them around the room, maybe while still holding onto the body. This was the worst yet.

There was nothing that we could do right now except observe. The scene had to be processed by John's men. John asked the sheriff if he knew who the victims were. He said the girl in the restroom was a seventeen-year-old high school student and the one outside was a forty-seven-year-old housewife. It appears that during the movie the seventeen-year-old went to the bathroom. There she was either met or joined by the killer. The older woman probably walked in or was about to walk in while this was going on. The chief directed us over to the ticket booth. While walking over, he told us that the woman outside was discovered by the ticket taker. It seems that while in the ticket booth, the young lady heard something like a knock on the back door. Being curious, she opened the door and looked around and saw the woman lying in blood outside the restroom. She quickly ran back to the ticket booth and called the police.

The chief said, "When we got here, we roped off the area and discovered this." He pointed to a pile of flesh about six inches long near the back of the ticket booth. It was the other half of the lady's face.

John told the chief that they had done a good job and that his men would take over now. He said he would still need them for crowd control. John instructed his men to increase the police lines another ten yards out and down the sidewalk.

As usual, they were hauling out massive amounts of equipment, including cameras, lights, testing equipment, with some of them donning white lab uniforms and boots. It looked like we were to be here for a while.

John said that he wanted to interview the ticket girl. While he was doing that, I started looking for footprints. I can see mine and John's coming out of the restroom easily, but every eight feet or so, there was another print. It wasn't a distinct set of prints because they were on the theater carpet. But you could make out that they were the same type of large padded canine footprints. I pointed out the prints to John's men, and they put markers out so no one would step on them.

One of those footprints—the last one on the carpet—looked like it had torn a four- or five-inch piece of carpet loose. Then going in the same direction ten or fifteen feet out until we hit the sidewalk, there were no more prints I kept looking, and about twelve feet more out on the sidewalk was something that looked like a smudge of blood from a footprint. This could be where he leaped twenty-five feet out of the theater. There were no other traces of him touching the sidewalk and that was the only logical premise. Of course, John's men documented all the findings.

I asked John if the ticket girl that seen anything. He said not really. After the knock on the ticket booth door, which was part of that woman's face hitting the back door, she thought she saw something out of the corner of her right eye; something big and black streamed by. She didn't even think it was real until she was pressured for more information about it.

By that time, relatives of the victims had showed up and were making a big commotion at the police line. The chief excused himself, saying that this was part of his job. John and I watched as he went over to talk to and console the victims' relatives and friends. It was a small town and news travels fast. Pretty soon, there was more than twenty people who were either relatives or friends. They all needed some reassurance. The closest relatives were trying to break through the police lines to see their loved ones. We knew that was something they really didn't want to do.

After all the commotion was over and we were just waiting around for them the process the scene, John suggested that we go over to the diner nearby for some coffee. So John and chief and I walked about fifty yards over to the local diner. It was pretty much past dinnertime, and we were all probably pretty hungry. We took a booth, and John started a lighter conversation with the chief about how long he was there and what type of experience he had.

Basically, he was a small-town cop his whole life, being chief the last ten years. He was in his sixties and had no plans for retirement, until maybe today. He said in thirty-five years of law enforcement, he's never seen anything close to that. He said he'd been in the war and seen bodies blown apart but that it was beyond his imagination to think of what did that to that poor girl. John quickly chimed in, "We call it a serial killer. I've been on its trail three and a half years. He's killed like this before and will probably continue until we stop him." John also said it would be a good idea if the chief informed all this men that we use the term *serial killer* for this perpetrator. "We don't want to have a panic of the population. So, for now, just refer to it as a serial killer."

The chief said "Got it," and excused himself to go to the men's room.

While John and I were alone, I asked him, "Is this the way this serial killer acts, tearing his way through humanity?"

John said, "This is the first time he's done two in a row. Most of the time, he pops up every three to five months somewhere in the Northwest. It has been hard to track him. The trail always ends abruptly. He leaves no clues as to where his next victim might be. All the information we have suggests it's the same person."

I looked at him real funny and said, "No person could do that."

John said, "We refer to it as a person but, believe me, we're covering all bets in our investigation and pursuit."

I looked John again and said, "I hope you don't get mad at me for asking you this. Does the word *werewolf* ever come into the conversation?"

He said, "We don't use that term because of obvious reasons. But, as I said, we are covering all bets."

Then I asked about little June—the girl who had been injured in the previous attack. He said she was being well taken care of and that she would be under observation for a while to make sure she had no ill effects from her encounter. He also said that her closest relative was a single uncle who lives about thirty miles away. Although he didn't get involved in this part of the investigation, there was some question as to it being in her best interest to go live with her uncle or a more suitable foster family. I said, "Well, sounds like she's doing as a good as possible."

John had a few questions to me about my work at the college doing autopsies for the state police. He said I could spend a few more days with his group to see how they process the information back in the lab. I said I wouldn't mind at all. It would be very interesting and helpful for me when I finally got back to work after my sabbatical.

The chief made it back. The waitress came over and asked what we'll have and we all said in unison, "Coffee."

After about fifteen minutes and a lot of small talk between the chief and John, we all decided to get a substantial meal. After that, John said he got me a room at a local hotel. It seems his whole crew was staying there. I ended up on the third floor with either side of my room taken up by John's crew. I didn't mind too much because they were very quiet, and guards were posted outside in the hallway all night long. It made me wonder exactly how dangerous this investigation is going to be. But we were on the third floor and there were guards outside all night, so how much danger is there?

Next morning started early. The men were processing all the evidence. They were doing computer checks and comparing past evidence that has been collected. It took about six hours for them to confirm that it was the same perpetrator. John called in some additional men to continue the search for the SUV that we had identified where the trail stopped previously. We were in a small town, but they still felt it would take a couple of days to check out all the cars.

John had the state police check if there were any similar vehicles registered in this town or in the surrounding areas. What I really saw them doing was basic everyday police work with a little bit of laboratory evaluation thrown in.

It looked like the investigation was ending and most of the work that was to be done here had been done. Then all hell broke loose. The police chief ran up to the vehicle which housed the control center of the operation and told one of John's men that a young girl had just been discovered missing on the other side of town. She and her family lived in what the chief described as the projects or low rent part of town. The call had come in less than five minutes ago, and the chief wanted to alert John on the way over. John signaled his two top men to come with him, and they all ran over to the chief's car to get in. I ran along and asked if I could come.

John reached in his pocket and threw me the keys to his car and said "Sure, follow us in my car," and then he said "There is a loaded shotgun in the backseat." I figured we had to be ready for anything, right?

I follow the chief's car with the siren blasting, running through red lights, getting to the other side of town. I know they call this area the projects. To tell the truth, these were nice little condos. They were not anywhere near what I have come to know as the projects. The mother was outside with one of the local police and was very upset. John, the chief, and his men parked, ran over, and started questioning her. I saw John through the car window. From what I had learned from him, he was getting all the facts so he could launch an intelligent and efficient search. I knew I wasn't going to be of help there, so I thought I'm going to take a look around. After all, if this was the same perpetrator, then we knew where he had been. But the idea is to get ahead of this killer.

These project buildings held about thirty townhouses, upstairs and downstairs. Just down the street from the entrance of this missing girl's home was a large parking lot with about 300 cars and about fifty or sixty yards across the parking lot was a field a hundred yards wide which ended at the edge of the woods. I drove around the block once. It was dinner time and there was practically no one out. I drove past the house again where John was still questioning the mother. I thought I would take a look in the parking lot. After all, there were a lot of cars there and there were a lot of spaces in between them.

I slowly drove into the middle parking lot and parked the car, got out, opened the back door, and took out the shotgun. Well, you never know what you might find. I thought it was best to be prepared. I was in my hunter mode now. I started poking around, looking in between cars up and down the aisles to see if anyone else was in the parking lot. I couldn't see anyone else except John, his men, and the chief about one hundred yards away down the street. I continued to go down each aisle looking *in* between the cars. I was looking and listening and trying to take up any sense or clue as to the disappearance of this little girl. Like when I was hunting in the field, I would go five to ten steps, stop, pause, listen, look, and then go on when I was sure that I had covered the area. I had done the procedure ten or fifteen times when I was moving through a couple of parked cars and entering another aisle. It was then that I heard something from across the adjacent parking aisle. It sounded like someone slurping up eggs that weren't well done. Occasionally, it sounded like lips smacking, like the person was enjoying their meal. This wasn't a sound you would expect in a parking lot. I looked around and over the tops of the cars and didn't see anything. I quietly walked down my side of the aisle. I was looking in the direction of the sound. There were two rows of cars across from me parked front to front. It was when I had gone down looking between the parked cars that I noticed something. I was looking across the aisle, about 30 feet and down the length of two parked cars. It wasn't clear at first, so I bent down and lifted my glasses to focus better in order to make out what was sticking out from behind the furthest car.

I must've looked at it for about eight seconds when I realized what it was. It was an animal's leg—hairy and almost human. It had a massive calf muscle about as big as my thigh. I couldn't see the knee, but about four feet was sticking out from behind a van. What was most interesting was that it had a very unimpressive heel. The major part of the foot, which was about fifteen inches long, was on the front pad and toes which were touching the roadway. He looked like he was leaning over one foot in front of the other, doing something that was making the noises. I don't know why I focused on his foot so much. It's just that I've never seen anything like it before. Here I am finally facing a killer and I'm more interested in his foot than what the rest of him is doing.

Well, I finally got over my astonishment, amazement, or whatever you want to call it, and I raised my shotgun up and clicked off the safety. Instantly, the leg vanished. I ran across the parking aisle and decided to skip a car space, just in case he was waiting for me behind the van. When I peered around the car, I could see what he was doing. There was a little girl's body on the roadway. She had been mutilated like the one in the cabin. I quickly looked up and could see a large animal running on all fours across the field. I went to shoot at it, and to my amazement, just before it went to the woods, it stood up on its two feet, made a right turn, ran about twenty feet while looking at me, and then jumped into the woods. I just stood there, partly dumbfounded, partly mesmerized. I started to think I should have shot at him. Even though this all took place about one hundred yards away, I really thought I should have shot at him.

My eyes then went back to the little body lying on the ground. Now I know what those sounds were that I had heard. It was him eating.

I took another look at the child. It looked like he was holding her up against the van while he was raking flesh off her back. There was a lot of blood around in that area. She was probably killed and bled out there, also. A young, freshly killed, mutilated child is not a pretty sight to see. It drains something from you. To be more specific, it drains life and goodness from you. You can never be the same afterward. I had that same sick angry feeling that I had when I saw the girl in the cabin. I had to tell John what had just happened.

I called John on the cell and told him that I had found the girl and not to bring the mother. The first one at the scene was a state trooper. He jumped out of his car and started running at me with a rifle, yelling for me to put down my firearm. I guess he didn't know I was the one who found the child. I left the shotgun on the car and stepped several yards away with my hands in the air. As soon as he got close to me, I explained that I was the one who found the child and notified the authorities. John and his men drove up in the chief's car and immediately took control. People were starting to come out of their homes to check out what all the excitement was. John told his men and the state trooper not to let anyone in the parking lot and that this whole area was a crime scene. John said to me, "Show me the girl."

As we were walking over, I explained what happened and what I had seen. John seemed very interested in the fact that I had been within thirty to forty feet of this animal. When we got to the girl's body, John shook his head and said that he didn't know what's going on because a killer had never been this active before. It looks like he's really coming out. I said quietly to John, "I saw this thing's leg up close. I saw him run on all fours and on two legs. He's covered with hair and larger than a 700-pound bear. Do we have a name for him yet?"

John said, "Yes, he's a serial killer."

Pretty soon, several other police cars and the rest of John's crew arrived. They started putting up drapes and covering around the body so no one could see the corpse and what they were doing. It was going to be a full night of samples, pictures, and processing evidence. The girl's mother arrived, dragging the police chief with her. He had been trying to hold her back at their townhouse. She was crying and screaming that she wanted to see her daughter, and wanting to know why they wouldn't let her see her daughter. Just to be sure, John called over the state trooper, and we issued the order that no one was to enter the parking lot until we finished processing the area. The trooper said there was a guy who wanted to get his car out to go to work that evening.

John said, "No one comes in. Nothing leaves the area."

The trooper said, "Gotcha."

By this time, several of the neighbors were helping to calm the distraught mother. The chief was busy with crowd control, trying to get people to go back into their houses and answering questions as to what was going on. He kept telling people there was a serial killer on the loose and that they should all go home and lock themselves inside. They were concerned for their safety, and rightly so.

The chief said he and his men would be doing patrols all night long. John had moved his command center into the parking lot. He was in touch with the state police and asked them if they could send more cars and troopers to help patrol the area. I guess he didn't think the local police force was really up to this type of operation.

It took about six more hours to process the area and the body. During this time, about six TV news vehicles showed up and started interviewing people and reporting as to what they thought was going on. No one working on this case would allow themselves to be interviewed. John said we would be staying at the same hotel, in the same rooms, and that he had made all the arrangements. He said that he needed some time to talk to me after dinner. Of course, I agreed. As we were leaving, I asked if we would be using the dogs in the morning. John said he was thinking about it. Little did we know that that was not going to be an option. Later, we were to find out that the governor was going to get involved and he was going to send in the cavalry in the form of the National Guard.

We all drove together to the same diner that we had gone to before. The eating arrangement was the same—we all set in the center of the room in a circle so that everyone had a view of everyone else's back. One individual ate apart from the rest. His back was up against the wall and he had in view of the whole dining area. I noticed this time that he had an MP 500 in his jacket. That's a short-barreled automatic .223 rifle used for close encounters.

These guys weren't taking any chances. They were always well protected. I didn't mind the arrangement because it got us in a more sociable arrangement where we had plenty of the investigative group around me to discuss their thoughts and observations on what was happening. We were there fifteen minutes when the chief of police came in and told John that the governor had sent for the National Guard to come in and search the adjacent woods. It seems someone higher up thought that it would be a good thing for the state to get involved and show its concern. The military might take up residence in the area. John just shook his head and said, "They don't know what they're getting into."

After dinner, we all walked over to the hotel. The arrangement there was also the same—room third floor, with his men occupying rooms to either side of. I was in my room for ten minutes until John knocked at the door, wanting to talk to me. I kind of thought this was going to be my termination meeting with the group. I had been allowed to do and see more than any civilian.

John came in carrying a leather bag. I could see it had more in it than just papers. He set it down next to the table of my room and asked me to take a seat across the table. He took a seat on the opposite table and pulled the back up next to his chair. Then he started to talk, saying, "As you know, I have been on the trail of this serial killer for a few years now. He has never left any witnesses alive. In fact, he has killed everyone that has even come close to him or has seen his work. Right now, I have a little girl who has seen him and she is being held at a secure military installation far from here. I don't know how or why it is that you have seen him more than once and are still alive. It is our feeling that he will hunt you down and kill you and anyone close to you at the time. As you know, we had been keeping you pretty close these past few days. But unknown to you, we've had twenty-four-hour surveillance on your family at your home.

"We weren't sure about how we could continue to protect you, but when we considered your aptitudes and your abilities, we thought it would only be fair to give you a chance to hunt and fight against the thing that is hunting you. We want you to join us. You'll be on the government payroll, just like all of us. Your family will continue to be protected, and if we feel they are in more danger, they will be put in protective custody. I want to know how you feel about this offer."

At first, I was very surprised that they would even consider me as part of the group. But then I thought about the security issues for my family and myself, and I knew there wasn't any other way *to* go. Then I said *to* him, "I think it's a very good idea."

He said, "Good. We will be issuing you firearms. You will be able to carry them concealed in any state of the union. I want you to have these now." John reached into the black leather bag and pulled out several pistols. There was a .44 Magnum, a .45 auto and a .44 special short barrel. The first two had shoulder holsters and the third came with an ankle holster. He said they all were loaded with silver bullets, and in the bag there were several hundred rounds for each pistol. I reached over and grabbed the .44 Magnum. It was a Smith and Wesson. John said that he wanted me to take these firearms everywhere I went and that that was an order. He also said that I would be issued a rifle and shotgun some time next morning.

He also said that I would be working with Sam and Howard who were in charge of taking lab samples. My official title would be lab technician, and Sam and Howard would be my immediate supervisors. I told John that I knew Sam and Howard were in the room next to me on the right and when was it that I should report to them. He said that as soon as we finished our discussion, he would take me over there and tell them that I was on board.

John said that we needed to do some administrative work. He needed me to fill out a W-2 form and tell him what my salary was at the hospital because they were going to match it. He said because it was not safe for both his men and me to go home very often, the money would be sent to my wife and I would be given a monthly stipend deposited in a debit card which they would give me. He said this system of payment has worked well for everyone. He also said free health insurance was also included in this deal and that we could get medical care at any military hospital or installation in the country. Other than the fact that I would not be seeing my family very often, it seemed like a good deal, especially the healthcare part.

After all the paperwork was finished, we walked over to Sam and Howard's room, and John told them I was officially onboard. Just about that time, we could hear the National Guard trucks going down the street. John told us to find out where they were setting up. He also said he needed to talk to their commander to find out when and where they were going to deploy so we would not be duplicating our effort.

The team—consisting of me, Sam, and Howard—decided to leave in about ten minutes. I went to my room and strapped on the Smith and Wesson and ankle pistol. As I was leaving my room, I thought of how I was really in it now, being an official investigator. Then it quickly also occurred to me that this thing we were hunting wasn't going to let me be around that long. I had to call my wife to let her know I was not going to be home for a while. I was glad that the family was being protected and that I was not going to be around them. I knew now I had a target on my back. I was being hunted and I didn't want to be anywhere near them.

We found the National Guard bivouacked right next to the area between the parking lot and where I last saw the creature, or should I say serial killer, jump into the woods. Truckloads of soldiers were still coming in and setting up tents and a supply depot. We learned there was going to be a whole company, with all the support and supply they needed for the next three or four days. We found out that Capt. O'Connell was in charge of the operation, and we sent this message to John. John didn't waste any time in arranging a meeting with Capt. O'Connell. It seems that the captain planned to move out in the morning after breakfast, about 8:00 a.m. His company—about 250 men—was going to comb 600 to 700 acres of dense woods in an attempt to locate the perpetrator of these killings. He said if he's there, we'll find him. John suggested that his men comb in groups of four or five. The captain didn't think it was a good idea because they couldn't cover as much ground and the perpetrator might be able to slip between the lines of men.

We were out near the area they were bivouacked. They were a bunch of loud city guys. You could hear them three blocks away.

They were always talking and making wisecracks. I don't think there was a woodsman or hunter among them. They did deploy a perimeter of lookouts around the camp. All they did was walk and smoke. Not one of them stopped to look and listen in the woods. Well, what do you expect from weekend warriors? The next morning would turn out to be a real eye-opener for them and their officers.

On the way to breakfast the next morning, we saw them lining up. We couldn't really hear them talking but we could see them well enough. They were smoking, talking, and joking while they were waiting to be deployed by the captain. They came to attention as he strutted out onto the field in front of them. This was his big day; he was sending 250 or so men into the woods in search of the enemy. The last thing we saw was groups of men being led by their lieutenant and squad leaders charging into the woods. John just shook his head and said, "I hope they don't find anything."

The captain had ordered the lieutenants to have the men spread out as they walked through the forest. Each squad—led by a squad leader—was assigned a particular area to cover. All the slides were to advance in unison. They expected to be spread out with a distance of about ten yards between the men. The lieutenant pictured a uniform line of men advancing and combing the woods.

This was the plan, but in effect it didn't turn out that way. No one was monitoring the different types of terrain the men would be encountering. One group had it pretty easy going, while another squad was slowed down in briars and thicket. It wasn't too long until some squads were hundreds of yards ahead of others.

Some squads were split and others were concentrated because of impassible areas. The squad leaders would send runners back to the lieutenants to tell them they lost track of the adjacent squad they were to be traveling with. The lieutenants would send word back that they should continue on and meet up with the squad next to them when the forest got less dense. It never did.

The last squad on the right—about fifteen to twenty men—was progressing steadily through the woods. Most of the time, the members could either see or hear each other talking. They were a quiet group. Because they were the last squad on the end of a long line of men, it was easy to circle around in back of them, and that's exactly what he did.

He made it easy for himself. It was the easiest way to take casualties. The woods were fairly dense in that area; there was a lot of dense high undergrowth. In this area, the men were used to not seeing the man next to them for maybe ten or thirty feet as they push their way through bushes and tree limbs which made the progression forward very slow and laborious. He chose to start with the fifth man in on the right. The soldier never knew what hit him as he was fending his way through the underbrush. We knew that later by observing the look on his face when his body was found. It was the same with the next two soldiers. They look like they had been hit by a locomotive, with body parts torn off and intestinal contents thrown over the underbrush. It was a total surprise for them all. Their facial expressions were totally blank. They never knew what hit them.

With the last two soldiers, it was a different story. He wanted to be seen by them. He wanted their cries to be heard, and he wanted to alert many other soldiers with the firing of their rifles. This was what he wanted, and this is what he accomplished. When he attacked the next to the last man on the end, he took his time ripping and tearing into him, as the man screamed, fired his rifle, and yelled for help. There was no one there except the last soldier on the end of the line. I can only imagine his fear when there were finally no more cries and he got no response to his call to his fellow soldier.

It was the same for him—a lot of ripping and tearing and crying and firing and then silence. The squad leader, when he heard the commotion, gathered as many soldiers as he could, and they charged where they last heard the commotion. They showed a lot of bravery in their attempt to help their fellow soldiers. It was too late because from the beginning they never knew what they were up against. So now you can imagine their horror when they discovered their comrades' bodies. It was especially disconcerting as they approached the body of the last soldier because half of his torso was flung through the air at them. The squad leader was smart enough to know there was something there he could not contend with. He ordered his men to retreat and regroup with the other squads. He also sent a couple of messengers to tell the lieutenant what happened and to ask for more reinforcements in a more concentrated force.

It was about midmorning when the captain contacted John, asking for our assistance. He was just starting to understand that this just wasn't a normal killer. John told him not to touch anything at the scene. He said we would need an escort of about fifteen armed men and fifteen men to help carry our supplies and lab equipment to the scene. John said he wanted to start in twenty minutes because he wanted to get a lot of work done before dusk. He didn't want anyone in the woods at nighttime.

John and fifteen investigators, including myself, with the captain and lieutenant and thirty soldiers hiked up to the scene. The rest of the day was spent ribboning off the areas around the bodies and finding various body parts in the dense foliage. About a half an hour before dusk, John had his men stop working, leave most of the equipment there, and return to the town.

The captain had his troops bivouacked in the field between the woods and a parking lot next to the town projects. He, all of a sudden, decided to regroup and bivouacked in the center of town at a park. From there, he and the state police patrolled the perimeter of the town. The state police patrolled in their cars, two officers in each car. The soldiers walked the perimeter in groups of five.

The captain, I think, was starting to face up to what he might be against. The center of town was definitely a safer site from which to deploy his soldiers.

By the time we got back to the inn where we were staying, it was dark and we still had to eat. We were staying at the same inn as the night before. The security was the same as the night before—two men on duty, one man stationed in the control center vehicle with cameras all around watching our cars and equipment. He had full view of our third-story windows to make sure no one was trying to gain an entrance to our sleeping quarters. The other man was stationed in the hallway on the third floor. He had full battle gear, including a battle helmet with a microphone. He was armed with an automatic rifle attached to a flashlight. There were two other lights with batteries facing opposite ways down the hall. He also had a motion detector that would detect any movement in the hallways and stairwells. It was a pretty safe area. No one was coming in or going out without our knowledge.

We had secured nine rooms for our team on the third floor. They were all on the same side of the building with their windows facing the same parking lot with our equipment. John had his own room with an adjoining door going into my room.

This is how they were constructed. Every two rooms had a set of common adjoining doors. The doors could only be opened from inside your room. If you opened your door, you immediately were faced with a closed door going into the other room. These doors were more of social obstacles than protection. They were very flimsy and thin. They were not like the hallway doors which were solid wood with large locks.

John had to have his own room because he was always on the phone conducting the operation. I was always stationed next to him since I was the new guy and he wanted to keep an eye on me. I didn't mind this at all since our two rooms were always situated in the center of the building, with the rest of the men on either side of us. The armed guard in the hallway was right outside our rooms. It was a good plan and well orchestrated and maintained. And the management was told not to rent out any rooms on the third floor during our stay, so we never saw anyone else up there, not even cleaning people were allowed. John even had a sensor in his room which would notify him if anyone came in while he was away.

There was one point, though, that we overlooked. The last room on the right occupied by two of our men had an adjoining unoccupied room separated by those flimsy doors. With the windows and doors guarded, no one imagined a threat coming from that direction. Philip and Vincent were in that room. Both of these men had been with John from the beginning. These were men who did everything by the book and slept with their guns next to them in bed. They never let their guard down. The next morning they were going to lead the group into the woods to finish collecting samples and decontaminating the area, whatever that means. Unfortunately, a lot of plans had to be remade that evening.

I was in bed and had just turned off the light when I heard the shotgun blast. The men in the room next to Philip and Vincent heard a crash, men screaming, and a shotgun blast. I immediately got my pants on, grabbed my loaded shotgun, and ran out into the hall. John and several other of our men were already banging on the door where the commotion had occurred. We were all ready to break in the door when Phil managed to crawl and unlock the door to the hallway. He then collapsed on the floor, bloodied and half conscious. Vincent was lying against the wall by his bed, unconscious. We could see where something or someone had burst through the doors adjoining the rooms. Not only had burst through the door, but it had taken the frame and part of the concrete support with it into the room. You can see where Philip had been thrown into the corner, with blood smears on the wall and a trail of blood leading to the hallway door. Both men seem to have serious injuries but they did not appear to be life-threatening. John called for the first aid kit, as two men started to work on Phil, and myself, John, and another saw to Vincent.

Phil was mumbling incoherently and pointing to the hole where the door was supposed to be. He was wearing his shoulder holster over his T-shirt. This pistol was on the other side of the room. It looked like he had been clawed on his right arm and left side. There appeared to be a bite mark on the left upper quadrant of his chest.

Vincent, who had been thrown across the room, striking his head on the wall, started to regain consciousness. He had a large clawed area from the top of his right shoulder down to his elbow. He also had a large bite mark on the apex of his right shoulder between the root of his neck and his deltoid muscle.

Once he got his senses about himself, Phil described all he remembered as to what happened. They had both decided to turn in

41

for the night, and Phil walked over to turn off the television. It was located against the wall next to those adjoining doors. He remembered a blast with something striking him and throwing him with the force of being hit by an automobile. The next thing he remembered was hearing people banging on the door and asking if everything was okay. He remembered how hard it was for him to crawl and unlock the door, being hurt all over and in shock. He finally started to realize what had happened to him when he looked at us bandaging his claw and bite marks.

Vincent, on the other hand, had seen most all of what happened. When Phil went to turn off the television, a giant animal burst through the door, picked him up, took a bite out of him, and slung him like a doll against the wall. Vince was struck by the door and pieces of concrete which stunned him a little but he managed to reach down and pick up a shotgun. He didn't get a clear shot because the animal was on him too quickly. The animal brushed the gun away, and he ended up firing into the ceiling. He remembered trying to get away and having his right arm raked. The animal's had picked him up and bit him between his neck and shoulder. Then he was tossed into the corner where he hit his head and went unconscious. The next thing he remembered was our administering smelling salts to help him regain consciousness.

John was already out in the hall arranging for ambulance transportation for his men to an unknown facility. This appeared to be a really big deal because he had two more live individuals who have been contaminated. They needed special transportation by special personnel to a secret specially-equipped facility which could handle their problem. He also called the local ambulance squad to come in and stabilize the men with intravenous solution because of their blood loss. After the local ambulance squad left, it still took two hours for the special ambulance to arrive and take the men away. During that two hours, the men seem to be suffering more from mental anguish than from their physical injuries.

It was Phil who started first. He started making statements about how his life was over and how he should've been killed because he knows what they do to people who are contaminated. A couple of the men tried to calm him down by telling him it was going to be all right and that he was going to get good treatment. But he kept saying, "This is it, man. This is it. This is the end."

I turned to a couple of the other investigators and asked what he meant by that. They just turned and walked away.

Vince was a little more stoic. He kept saying things like "Tell my family I love them" "Make sure they're safe" and "Don't let them know what really happened." We tried to calm him down as best we could, telling him that he was going to be able to tell his family himself and that these injuries were not that severe.

I have to say I was very disturbed and taken aback by what I was seeing. Here, we have a couple of heroic men who have survived a terrible attack, and they're not very happy about their future. Apparently, they had some information that I had not been allowed to have. I thought I'd ask John what was going on with them.

John was just getting off the phone when I approached him. I told him what I had seen and what I had heard from his men. Then I asked him straight out, "They don't exterminate contaminated people, do they? Is little June still alive?"

John looked very pensive and asked me to come and sit down with him in an empty room. He said that June was the first person to survive an attack. Until her case, they had no way of knowing if this disease or contamination could be passed on to another person. June had to be sequestered and watched for a period of time to see if there was any contamination. There were some signs in June in her hematological picture. There were changes seen. He said, "We'll be looking forward to the next full moon to see if there any more changes in her. The worst case scenario would be she would have to be taken care of in a secure facility the rest of her life. This would not be a jail cell but a nice facility where she would have grounds privileges but she would have to be watched the rest of her life so there could be no more contaminations with her blood."

So I asked John, "What your men fear is that they may become werewolves and they will have to be sequestered so they don't spread the disease?"

John said, "That's part of it. But, remember, these men are dedicated hunters They have been part of the investigation from the beginning. They want to be part of bringing this thing to an end. There is a lot of disappointment here."

I said I understand. I said to John offhandedly, "It's interesting. He usually kills, why did he leave both men alive?"

John said, "I haven't figured that one out, yet."

Then I had a thought. I asked, "You're not sending them to the same facility as June, are you?"

He said, "Why?"

Then I said, "If he follows the ambulance, they will lead him to where she is and he might want to finish all of his work there."

John looked at me in surprise and said, "I think you're right."

John immediately grabbed his phone and started making arrangements to reroute the injured men to a different location this time. It seems he was going to have them lifted by air to a more distant hospital. This suggested to me that if he was going to send them to the same facility with little June, it wasn't in driving distance. John was intense, punching numbers into his iPhone, making calls and arrangements, jotting down schedules and pickups. I thought as I looked at him, *Yes, he is a great administrator and leader, but I wouldn't want his job.* Most of the time he's on his phone or computer, punching keys or screens and reading emails. Then there's the constant reports to the higherups. For myself, I really prefer to be doing work in the field or lab. I like to get my hands into the job and really develop the outcomes.

From what I could hear from John working in the hallway, he had arranged for a medical helicopter to pick up the men and deliver them to an army hospital several hours away by air. This would definitely stop anyone who was following the ambulance by car. As I had said once before, this group of men appear to be very efficient and try to cover all outcomes.

Just as John was finishing up, Howard, who I was assigned with, notified John that just beyond the woods where the soldiers were killed there was a state park. The weekend was coming up and there would be a lot of campers in the woods. It was less than ten miles before you arrived at the park. The campers were not aware of our problem and had no protection. And if anything happened, it could be days before the incident was discovered.

John immediately said to Howard, "You and Dr. Blaine get on it right away. I want the park shut down over the weekend and next week. I want a meeting with all the camp rangers to inform them that we have a serial killer on the loose and the precautions should be taken to protect the public and the rangers themselves. I want the park shut down today and the meeting tomorrow. Get on it."

John knew how to assign about a weeks' worth of work into one day and night. They immediately started to look up all the parks in the area and devise methods of notifying their supervisors and directors of the immediate park closings. Luckily, the local police had a lot of these numbers in case of emergencies.

It was soon discovered that there were about twenty campers already using the park. We put into motion and an operation where the rangers would go out and notify the campers that they had to leave immediately because of a serial killer on the prowl. Luckily, there were more than enough rangers to actually escort campers out of the park. The location of the campers was known because they had to register at the main ranger station as to where they would be camping. It was at this ranger station that we set up the meeting in the middle of the next afternoon.

Howard and I were to go with some extra rangers and sweep the areas roads ten to fifteen miles out for any stragglers or unregistered campers. I was assigned three rangers and two vehicles. These vehicles were large official-looking Chevy Blazers, white, with the word *Rangers* on the sides. All the Rangers were armed with sidearms—9 mm hard plastic type of handgun. I don't think any of them ever had to use their sidearm, but the job called for it since they occasionally had to confront armed hunters and unruly campers miles from any police help.

Morris was in one Blazer, and Scott and Jim accompanied me in the other. We were hitting all the popular places the next morning where people camped and kids threw parties. Morris was assigned a few of the less popular areas and he was supposed to meet us back at ranger headquarters when he was finished.

We were visiting a few campgrounds which were further away. The Blazers were equipped with radios so we could keep in touch. About 11:30 a.m., Morris reported that he was on his way back to headquarters. We had one other place we wanted to visit, and then we were going to go back, also.

We had reached our final destination when Morris came over the radio. He said that he had had an accident, that something had hit his blazer and knocked him into a gully. He said the side of the gully was too steep and he could not drive out. He asked us to come pick him up.

I immediately became concerned for Morris's welfare. I told Jim, who was the senior Ranger and the one on the radio, to tell Morris to lock the doors and for no reason get out of his vehicle. I told him to tell Morris to just sit tight and we would be there as soon as possible. The last we heard from Morris was when he said he thought something was out there in the woods.

The rangers knew where this location was. It was one of the only spots where the road on one side went down into a gully about twenty feet deep which ended in thick undergrowth and woods. I told Scott, who was driving, to get there as quickly as possible because this did not sound good.

We got there in about five minutes. The Blazer was pointed down headfirst on a 60-degree slope of mostly rock and sand. We called out to Morris but there was no answer. It looked like the driver's door was opened about four inches. The slope was so severe that one couldn't walk down without sliding. And if you had to come up quick, well, you probably wouldn't. I told him to get a rope and that I would go down and investigate. We tied the rope to the trailer hitch of the Blazer. I told Jim to stay in the Blazer with the engine running so he could pull me up quickly in case there was trouble.

It wasn't my intent to play hero but I was the only one with a sidearm containing silver bullets. The only briefing that they had had was that there was a serial killer in the area. Because they were not mentally prepared or armed properly for what they might find the gully, it was really for me to go down and see.

The rope they gave me was about one hundred feet long so there was a lot left over when I threw it down into the gully. With the rope in one hand and my pistol in the other, I eased myself down the slope to the Blazer whose front bumper was resting against some small trees at the end of the slope. The slope was a little less steep at the end, so I dropped the rope and peered into the Blazer.

The passenger window had been broken in with glass all over the front seat. There was blood all over the front seat, and Morris's body was resting on the floor in front of the seat. The door had been sprung, like something had ripped it open without using the handle. I had to pull the door open to get to Morris. He was lying away from me. I reached in and checked his dorsal pedal pulse and popliteal pulse on his leg. They were both absent. Further inspection revealed that his throat was torn apart. His pistol was on the far end of the passenger seat. It looks as if he didn't get a chance to use it. I yelled up to the men, "Morris's body is here! He's been killed."

Both Jim and Scott started yelling questions down to me, "What the heck happened here? Who could have done this?"

I wanted to take a look at the other side of the vehicle. I pulled myself up the rope across the back of the Blazer and down the other side. The passenger door was pushed in about six inches where it had been hit. I looked closely and could see some long gray brown hairs caught in the door and on the sideview mirror. I went back to the other side of the car and looked for footprints. There they were. Those large canine footprints that I had learned to recognize. I climbed back up to the road where the Rangers were waiting by the Blazer.

Jim asked, "What knocked him into the gully? We didn't see any other vehicles. It must've been a big one. And why didn't he have a chance to fight back?"

I said to both of them, "It doesn't appear as if his SUV had been struck with another vehicle and he didn't have a chance to fight. And what I think is the most important thing for us to do now is to notify the proper authorities to come out and process the murder scene. I think we should drive back to ranger headquarters immediately and use that area as a staging ground."

It was just then that I remembered that I hadn't notified anyone about what just happened. I should have notified John immediately when there was a sign of trouble so he and his men could have been on their way over to assist us. Thinking I'll do that right now, I grabbed for my phone.

Just then, the rope which I used to climb down the slope went taut and pulled out the Blazer about six inches toward the gully. Before we got over our astonishment and surprise, the Blazer was again pulled; this time about a foot and a half toward the gully. I said to Jim, "Let's get out of here."

Just as we were getting in the SUV, it was pulled another two feet toward the gully. Jim pushed the accelerator all the way down in low gear, and we didn't move except to drift closer to the gully. Then we were pulled again. It was only three or four more feet and our back tire would have been over the edge. I jumped out of the passenger side and ran to the back to try to untie the rope. It was impossible. The knot was to tight I raised my pistol toward the woods where the rope extended. It was about six feet off the ground, extending way out into the woods, using all that one hundred feet of rope. The SUV was pulled again closer to the edge. Jim was gunning the car, and the wheels kept spinning but we weren't going anywhere. We were pulled again, and I raised my pistol to shoot the rope. Scott beat me to it with his hunting knife and cut the rope. We jumped in the SUV and took off.

We were all sweating and shaking with fear. I had to tell Jim to slow down a little to a safer speed because we didn't want any accidents which would strand us on the road. They were saying things like "What the hell was that?" "What could do something like that?" "Was that what got Morris?" I told him, "Yes," about Morris and that the rest of the questions would be answered at the briefing this afternoon. But right now I had to make emergency call to my boss.

I got John on the phone. He was very serious about what had happened, especially the part about losing one of the rangers. Instead of immediately sending out a crew to process the site, he thought it was best that we have a meeting with all the rangers and explain to them exactly what we were up against and how dangerous the situation had become.

When we arrived at ranger's headquarters, there were about fifteen rangers there. By the solemn look on their faces, John had already told them that they had lost a man. We were very sad-faced when we got out of the car and walked up to the headquarters ourselves. There were also about ten of John's investigators at the meeting, with several more arriving during the session. John got right on it. He called the meeting to order as soon as we walked in. He didn't try to sell the concept of serial killer anymore. He just used the word *beast.*

The first thing he wanted to do was to make sure the park was completely cleared of humans. He made up five patrols consisting of three rangers and one of his men. He said special high-powered rifles would be issued to all of the men who were in the park area. He made one very strict rule—no one was to be in the park between dusk and dawn. All operations would be conducted during daytime. This would also include the processing of the latest victim.

There were a lot of hands going up all over the room with a lot of questions, like "What kind of beast is this?" "Why do we need high-powered rifles?" "How big is he, anyway?" and "Is this the animal that killed Morris?"

John said, "Yes. He is extremely fast and powerful. You'll know him when you see him. You will be further filled in by your escort. I want the groups to leave now on a search and rescue before dark. As you leave the building, you will be issued your rifles. It is extremely important that no one else is left in the park tonight."

Immediately, the investigators, who were going to escort the rangers, picked out their three-man groups and left. John immediately gathered the rest of his investigators, including me and the two rangers with me, and outlined the way we were to process the last victim. He was interested in the general lay of the land, the denseness of the forest, and how to best protect his men as they process the area. He concluded that we should have at least five men with automatic weapons protecting the area at all times. He asked the rangers if they would accompany his men to show them the site. He wanted them to leave right now and start the processing, knowing that it would probably not be completed until the next day. He stressed that they must be out of the park and back at ranger headquarters before dark.

John said the ranger headquarters would be the command center for this operation, and we would be spending the night there. By this time, ten or more of our investigative team had arrived. A couple of men were assigned security of the rangers headquarters and were instructed to put floodlights around the whole area with guards.

I thought I was going to go with the men to process the site, but John quickly told me that together he and I were going to work with the state police to section off the park and see if there were any suspicious vehicles in the area. This was going to be accomplished with a couple of helicopters and about six state police vehicles traveling around the perimeter of the park. John already had maps laid out, with the state police captain waiting in another room to assign his troopers areas to control. There were still four or five hours till dusk, and we were going to make good use of the time.

Just then, one of the helicopters was landing at ranger headquarters to pick us up. John motioned to me to get on board and started to the door himself. Just before he exited the building, he turned to the state trooper commander and told him it might be a good idea to notify the police departments of any surrounding towns that there is a killer on the loose. Then we got into the helicopter and took off.

Once we got to our observational height, we could see about five miles in any direction. We were using binoculars and had satellite feed since it was a clear day. This was an immense park with a lot of dirt roads that ended at campsites. The perimeter, however, was lined by highways that were easy to follow. There were very few cars on the highways; so few that the state troopers could stop and question everyone. No one suspicious was found. They must've stopped about twenty cars but no SUVs with a single individual inside. So about dusk, we were dropped back to ranger station. As we were exiting the helicopter, John pulled me over and told me he needed to talk to me later that evening.

Whenever John has a special meeting with me, I have come to learn that there have been new developments which involve me specifically. I was a little anxious about what he was going to say, but there was a lot to do still.

Everyone was back from their searches of the area. The state troopers and rangers were dismissed, and we started to make plans at the ranger station that evening. It was the same drill—floodlights covering the surrounding area and four or five armed sentries with motion and heat detectors. We would be sleeping inside the station with sleeping bags on the floor. I would have preferred a soft hotel bed, but we had to stay near the command center since messages were coming and going constantly. It in itself was a twenty-four-hour operation, and we had to be there to run it.

Just before I turned in, and John asked me to take a walk with him. He said that there had been some new developments with June, the girl who was initially injured when I became involved in all this. He was going to visit and talk to her and he wanted me to accompany him. She was about 600 miles away at a military installation. He also said that since we were leaving the area, it would be a good opportunity for us to visit with our significant others. He said he could have my wife and two girls flown in to meet with me for a couple of days. With all the action and commotion, I hadn't thought much about them. It did seem like a pleasant idea, though. I asked John if he was going to visit with his family, also, and he quickly looked at me and said, "It's not a good idea to talk about your family or anyone else to anybody in this group. They could be captured, and they can't tell what they don't know." Once again, I was shocked back into the reality of our situation. Not only were we hunters, but we were being hunted.

It was hard getting to sleep. I had a lot of thoughts in my head, and even though it was 11:00 p.m., I could not fall asleep. I wondered what my wife would say after us not seeing each other for so long. I felt guilty that I had taken this job on and cause them to be in danger and without my immediate protection. I knew they had guards and were being watched, but I wasn't there. After all, I'm the man of the house and the primary responsibility for their safety rests with me.

Alone in the dark on that sleeping bag, I had some really bad feelings about what I should be doing and where I should be.

We were there two more days processing and cleaning up our case. Then we flew out for our family visitation. I was a little worried about how it would go until, upon seeing me, the whole family threw their arms around me and wouldn't stop kissing me. I did feel a little better then, and we had a great couple of days dining out, going to the movies, and having some real quality time talking

They were very inquisitive about what I was doing. I told them that I really couldn't talk about the investigation but that we were really close to catching a serial predator. The big question my wife has was how much longer it was going to take. I tried to calm her down by saying it would be a little while. She told me it was scary having guards twenty-four hours around our property and there wasn't much privacy since they were followed everywhere they went. I told her it wouldn't be much longer and if they can just put up with it for little while. The girls added that it was hard, too, to have fun on a date when you knew there was a policeman watching you somewhere. I told them it would end soon, although deep inside I was happy they were still being guarded.

I was trying to be attentive and engaged with all their conversations about what happened since I saw them last and how things are going, but part of me was still wondering about little June and what had happened to her. I hope because of that I wasn't acting too distant. After all, this was supposed to the quality time to make up for my absence. When it was time to leave, we all kissed goodbye. My wife held me close and said, "Come back soon and come back safe."

There was a part of me that wanted to go back home with her, but I still wanted to finish what I had started.

June was staying in a research facility inside a federal prison located within a military base. To get into the inner part of the facility, we had to be escorted by guards and researchers who had to give voice recognition and handprints to computers to gain entrance. This place was very secure, and only about ten people knew about June and her condition.

Upon entering June's dormitory, the whole atmosphere of the prison changed. The area was well lit, with plenty of windows. There were a few laboratories and several offices. June's living area, even though surrounded by bars and steel doors, was very well lit and pleasant-looking. The immediate supervisor of the day told us we had an office reserved for us to talk to June. It was located outside her secure living area, but he related that she was of no danger to us since the full moon was several weeks away. This told me right away that she was contaminated; she was a werewolf.

The doctor in charge said he wanted to talk to us before our meeting with June. He thought it was important for us to know who or what we were interviewing. He said June's IQ was off the charts and that he was incapable of judging how high her IQ was with today's instruments. He also said that her physical strength is three or four times that of a ten-year-old, even though she no longer looked ten years of age. Most astounding, he said, was her insight into human motives and desires through a minimal amount of conversation. He said she can see right through you. He also volunteered that, as of present, they are able to manage her very well at that facility, but as she grows older and stronger, they would not be able to ensure her safety or their own safety in the future. We thanked him for his input and walked over to where June was sitting.

June was waiting for us in her living room which had an array of entertainment modalities like TVs, computers, games, including chess, Monopoly, and video games, too. I was surprised how much she had grown since I last saw her. I had remembered her as a young girl, about nine or ten years of age. Now standing in front of me was a young poised woman of about fifteen years of age. She reached her hand out to me, saying, "It's so nice to see you again, Dr. Jordan," and then again to John's, she said "Welcome, Agent Gilleland." She immediately took control of the meeting, saying that they, the authorities, would like us to meet in one of the interviewing rooms. She started walking toward the room before John and I even got out a hello. The day supervisor started to follow her, as we did, also.

The interviewing room was more like a conference room. There was a large wooden table sitting on a plush carpet with six or seven leather chairs around the table. There was a little sink in the corner with a microwave and small refrigerator filled with drinks. June walked right in and motioned for us to have a seat. The day supervisor excused himself, saying he had things to do. He closed the door, which was halfway glass, and we could see there was a guard posted outside.

John immediately started the conversation. He said that we were worried about her and that we wondered how she was doing and if this facility was meeting her needs. She smiled as if this was exactly what she wished to talk about. She said, "I'm doing well here, the people are friendly, and they supply my needs as best they can." She also said, "In case you were wondering, I'm safer here and probably anywhere else, since I know there is one out there who wants to kill me."

This was kind of a startling statement, and John immediately followed up with questions, "How do you know that someone wants to kill you.?"

She said, "Very simple. I can feel it, and I know that he knows that I'm the only one who could catch him, and when I'm older, probably kill him."

John and I just looked at each other in amazement. We had certainly got more than we had expected. Then John again asked, "Is there any way we can make you more safe?"

June said, "Yes. Have all the guards chamber to their pistols with .44 Magnum silver bullets. I also need a button to push in my living quarters, which will lock down this whole facility, in case he makes his way in. That way, if he gets me, he won't get out."

John said, "I will start to work on this immediately."

June turned to me and asked, "Do you have any questions for me, Dr. Jordan?"

Well, I had had many questions, like wondering how she was doing but they had already been answered. Now, after the initial part of our visit, the information that I had heard and seen had not even reached the point of conjuring a question in my mind. The first thing I did get out was, "How have you healed from your attack?"

She said, "Physically, I feel totally healed and there is hardly any scarring." She pulled down her blouse, showing me her shoulder and part of her back, and there was nothing but a few thin white lines where there had been large deep claw marks. And she said, very solemnly, but in my mind, my emotions, and my soul, there have been extreme changes, "I'm just not the same as I used to be. What I perceive, hear, see, and understand is so much more than I could have imagined."

She went on, "As far as the mental and emotional trauma of that night, I still remember it, especially for the loss of my family, and I hate him for it. As for the horror of that night, since I am almost as capable of it as he is, it is not as startling as it was initially. I still think about what happened, and I have to accept it all—my increases strength, my superior mental abilities, my incomparable insight into this world, as well as pain and rage at the time of the full moon which is almost uncontrollable. I want to kill him for what he did to me and my family and for the fact that he is trying to kill me. I want to kill him because he wants to kill me because he's afraid of me. This is what I have to live with here. There is no one here capable of understanding me. There is no one like me here and no one with which to share my whole life experience." She looked out the window and the door and said, "The people here try to be friendly, but I know, to them, I am an experiment, a discovery they don't understand. I know I am capable of so much more than they suspect. I could escape from here, if I wanted, but I wouldn't last long on the outside with that one hunting for me. Right now, I want to be here. This is the safest place for me."

I was looking at John at that time but quickly went back to her and said, "I know this is hard for you, especially a young woman just beginning her life. Please understand it is very hard for us is to understand all your needs and how we can make your life as good as possible. You'll have to work with us on this."

John then said, "I think we have to have priorities here. I want you to be as safe here as humanly possible. I'm going to talk to the facility manager about the upgrades you mentioned before I leave today."

I again turned to June and said, "Do you think it would be helpful for you to have some young adults your age to visit and play games with?"

June shook her head and said, "Not really. That would be like me asking you to spend time playing with a bunch of newborns."

I shook my head yes, like I understood.

While she still had our attention, June asked, "Are there any other questions you would like to ask me?"

John and I both said that we had no more for now.

Then she said, "I have another request. I would like to help you find this killer. I think I could be very helpful if you would keep me appraised of his activities and the trail that he leaves. I would need a secure phone or means of communication that could never be traced back here. That's one reason I don't have an email. I know he's searching every possible means of communication to get a sense of me. I see a plan in his actions. He definitely wants to accomplish something, but he's displaying it as a game. He wants something from you or from one of you. He's drawing you in, closer and closer. He wants to keep your attention. He wants to have you come nearer and closer than ever before. He finds it exciting and creative to pull you in while all the while you think you are chasing him. You're hunting, but he's leaving the trail of blood that's so easy to follow. And you have to follow it, for, after all, isn't that your job, your duty, your dedication? It's like he has you on a string."

"We have to figure out what he really wants. I think it's more than just to shame the authorities and the police by showing he's so much superior. It's not ego food that he's after. There's a much deeper reason. After all, for one who has lived hundreds of years and would probably live hundreds more, what could be so intriguing and desirable as to cause him to come out and be known for what he is? He's willing to face the danger to get what he wants."

In the end she said, "I really hope you let me work with you. We will be able to save many more lives, including our own and lives of our loved ones. This creature is capable of anything you can imagine and then some."

John looked at me and said, "It sounds like a good idea, and we will certainly consider how we might bring it about. It will take some planning and approval from department heads, but I think it can happen. After all, we do use experts not in our profession to help us catch malevolent and bad people."

With that, she got up, and we started to follow. But just then, I thought of another question and I asked John if I could have a little more time with June. He said, "Yes," and walked out of the room, leaving us there. We both sat down again, and I looked at her and smiled, knowing that what I asked for may not be something I wanted to hear.

I said, "June, you seem to be more than what we are as humans. What do you think of us?"

She said, "You know, Dr. Jordan, I smelled something about you, but I didn't know what it was. I still don't know what it is because I've never sensed it before on a human, but I do know you're special. As far as humans go, you included, I think you are more wonderful and marvelous than you ever could imagine. You have no idea who you are. You think it relates somehow to your job, family name, your country, your wealth, your religion, or anything else you deem valuable and important. The truth is that these things, either singly or altogether, with which you identify and sometimes worship, they cannot support the full weight of your soul and who you truly are. You are too marvelous for words, and yet as a population, so blind. Do you know that even now there is enough food and wealth to feed everyone in the world? Right now, no one should be so hungry. Your only weakness that I see is that you think bad thoughts and believe them. You were created for a far better existence than you have."

I looked at her in amazement, and then I looked down because I just had to ask, "Is there a God?"

She looked down at me and said, "You had to ask? The whole world and all creation scream of His existence, and you can't hear. Look in the mirror. Look at life. Look at the love you have. Nothing in this world could create it, support it, and fulfill it, except God Himself. Everything else but Him will disappoint you. And all you want to do is to reason Him out of your lives and out of existence. You prefer to worship science which is nothing more than a figment of your imagination, a set of theories. That never have been proved and never will be proved. Even your theory of the *Big Bang* starts off not knowing where the matter for the big bang came from. I'll give you a little hint. It came from God. It was a condensation of His Spirit and Energy that made matter so reactive that it had to explode. This process might have happened several times. There is not enough information on the internet for me to figure that out."

I just stood there in complete wonderment. I had never been so defined, so edited and understood beyond my own understanding, and yet lifted up and held high beyond my wildest imagination. Little June certainly was more than I expected, more than I could ever be, and more than I could ever comprehend.

She was just standing there in front of me with a warm reassuring smile on her face. She knew who I was and she knew who she was, and even though it was so great a distance mentally in between, she didn't hesitate to speak the truth as she knew it.

After a little uncomfortable pause since I was still speechless, June reached out her hand to shake mine and said, "It was so nice having this conversation with you, doctor. I hope you come back again in the near future." With that, she took my hand, shook it, and led me toward the door, and she said, "Let me show you show you to the exit where your friends are waiting for you."

She was right; John was waiting for me at the exit door. He and I both said goodbye to June, and she quickly walked away back to her quarters as if she had some pressing projects which she had to complete. John looked at me and asked, "What did you and you talk about?"

I said, "John, it was the most amazing encounter that I've ever had in my life and I haven't quite wrapped my head around what she really said. I'd like to discuss it at a later date, if you don't mind."

He just smiled and shook his head yes, and we proceeded to walk the rest of the security doors and out to the car.

The next few days were spent in the main office. We did everything required to make sure we would be up to speed at our next investigation. That included ordering supplies and making sure all the vehicles were stoked with laboratory and investigative equipment, ammunition, communications equipment, and anything else we thought necessary for the next encounter. It wasn't long—less than a week—when we received an emergency call from a local police captain. This time, the killing was located about 250 miles north of our last investigation. We all left in together. John and I, with equipment and about ten other agents, left immediately in a couple of helicopters so we could quickly evaluate the scene. The rest of the agents came in the Suburbans and mobile lab.

The initial report from the police captain was that a young man, about thirteen years of age, went missing at around ten in the morning. He went out about nine o'clock after breakfast to play in his backyard which ends next to a 600- or 800-acre forest. It was reported that he often plays in the woods but is never out of earshot of his mother's voice. After about an hour of calling his name, his mother called the local authorities and reported him missing. They arrived with a couple of dogs and a five-man search team and found his body less than a quarter of a mile into the woods. When they called state police asking for help with this apparent homicide, they were quickly directed to our office after they described the appearance of the child's body.

It only took a couple of hours by air to reach the location. Property was a nice three- or four-acre spread out into the adjacent forest. When we landed, the police chief, whose name was John Timko, approached our helicopter and introduced himself. He volunteered that he and his men stayed away from the area as requested so they would not contaminate the same. He has been talking to the mother and father. The boy's name was Dino Ungarini. His dad's name was Temo, and his mother was called Maria. When we met them, they spoke with a deep Italian accent. The father had been working as a butcher in a meat market about thirty miles away in town. We could see that he was angry and agitated and wanted us all to go out and hunt for this predator that hurt his son. We assured him that that was definitely part of the investigation, but first we had to evaluate the scene.

Both John and I noticed several gun cases full of shotguns and rifles and a few pistols in the home. I walked up to one case and noticed a .44 Magnum Smith & Wesson, similar to my own. Temo came over to where I was standing. He related that he was an avid hunter who went out most evenings with his dogs hunting. He was no stranger to the forest or to the hunt, and he wanted to get his dogs and get moving.

Chief Timko said he would take John to the site. I thought it best if I stayed and talked to Dino's parents a little while longer because I got the feeling that his father was about to take off without us. While I was talking to them, I noticed there were several strings of garlic hung around the windows of their ranch.

Maria said that she was tying bunches of garlic and that it was good to hang around the house to ward off the evil eye. She also said that on the weekends she would rub a little garlic on Dino for his health and well-being. The school had asked her not to do it during the weekdays since the odor was very repugnant for the rest of his classmates and teachers. Being part Italian, I understood Maria. She was an Italian lady from the hills in southern Italy who had her own beliefs and practices. Temo, on the other hand, was a macho Italian male—five-foot-ten, 250 pounds of solid muscle. He was ashamed of the fact that he was not there to protect his son. In order to regain his honor and display his manhood, he had to go out and track down the one who had killed his son and hurt his family so bad. When he communicated, he talked with hand gestures more than with speech. I tried to explain to them that we had experience with these kinds of crime and that we were doing everything possible to find the killer. When I thought I had quieted them somewhat, I left to take a look at the crime scene.

The scene was about 250 yards into the woods. There was a little space between the trees and there lay Dino, a chubby thirteen-year-old lying face down, with his back muscles shredded down to the bone from his shoulders to his buttocks. It looks like it had been a quick kill with a quick bite to throat. John's men were busy taking pictures of footprints and taking samples of blood splatter. John thought it best if we just take the body back by stretcher for processing in the mobile lab since it was starting to get near dusk and he didn't want his men to be out there after dark. We weren't there more than an hour when John said "Let's go", and we loaded up little Dino on a stretcher and we all walked back together with a few of the local police and our investigators and guards.

The police chief had not been very talkative while we were processing the site. I think he felt way in over his head with this investigation. On the way back, he started asking some very familiar questions. He wanted to know what kind of an animal made those footprints and could do such a thing to a young boy. He also wanted to know if we had seen this type of thing before. John said that we had seen this before and that there is definitely a killer on the loose in the general vicinity. John told him that he should alert all the people living in the general vicinity that there is a killer on the loose and they should not go out alone at night. John also said he would alert the state police to increase their patrols in the area. John also told the police chief that there would be some special tracking dogs arriving in the morning and that he would appreciate as much manpower as the chief could spare for the hunt.

It wasn't quite dusk when we got back to the Ungarini home which was also our staging area of operations. Maria ran out to us as soon as we approached and told us that her husband had taken his guns and dogs and gone after the person responsible for this. John immediately turned to one of his organizers and said, "Get all the lights and equipment ready for a night hunt. We've got to find him quickly."

Tommy, the one he was speaking to, didn't look very happy to hear that they were going on a night hunt. As a matter of fact, he looked scared. And to tell the truth, I was a little frightened, having been in that woods where the trees were very close and there wasn't much space to maneuver. Just then, three quick shots, like those from a shotgun, rang out. They were followed by two pistol shots. John said, "We have to move now."

Chief Timko volunteered, "I want to come along."

John said, "Everyone who comes will need special armaments. We will issue them at the Suburban over there."

Just then, Tommy appeared with eight men carrying large floodlights. Each floodlight was attached to a battery strapped as a backpack to each man. The men carried floodlight in one hand and what looked to be like an automatic pistol, a MP 5 in the other hand. John was busy making sure everyone had proper weapons. He issued shotguns to the chief and two of his men who wanted to come along. I was given a shotgun, and the rest of his men were given automatic weapons and shotguns. The plan was we would proceed with one man with a light in the front and another man holding a light facing the rear. Two men would be shining lights on the left and the right. Each of these men with lighting would be backed up with three others carrying automatic weapons and shotguns. We would proceed in a tight group to work our way through the woods to where we heard the gunshots. Three additional men would proceed in the middle of the group and carry a stretcher and equipment. John orchestrated the whole procession, not letting anyone get too far ahead or fall too far behind. We were ordered to not let more than three feet separate each man.

We proceeded slowly into the dark woods. If you have ever been in the woods at night, you know that it's so dark that you cannot see your own hand right in front of your face. The floodlights gave us around a twenty-five-foot sight advantage, a lot more than a flashlight. We proceeded in the direction toward where we heard the sounds. The men didn't need much prompting to stay in a tight group. We didn't go more than 125 yards when two of Temo's dogs came up to us. They were pretty beaten up; one had its side clawed so badly that you could see its ribs. The other had had its jaw completely dislocated so it was torn free on one side. These were tough hounds—the kind you could hunt bear with—but they had been in a fight with something faster than a bear. They started the barking and making sounds at us and wanted to lead us back into the woods to help their master. We followed as quickly as possible.

We followed slowly for ten minutes or so, until they led us to a small clearing where we found both Temo's body and one of his dogs. It appeared that Temo knew how to hunt. He that two dogs trail the beast and had one on a leash to protect him in case the animal got between him and his chase dogs. And that's probably what happened. This smart wolf got around behind the dogs chasing him and went for Temo. The dog with him probably attacked the beast in an attempt to save his master. This gave Temo a chance to get off several rounds before being attacked.

Temo's body lay face up. There was a broken shotgun several feet from the body. His left forearm and hand were detached at the elbow and thrown fifteen feet away. Within inches of his stretched out right hand was a .44 Magnum pistol—the one I had seen earlier that evening in his gun cabinet. His main injury was a vicious bite to the left side of his neck.

John immediately told us to spread out around the body. He said he wanted 360-degree coverage with lights and guards. He told his operators to catch the two dogs who were still alive and put them on a leash and tie them to a tree since they were probably contaminated. He then went to Temo's body. There was a lot of blood on his shirt around his abdomen. Since there were no apparent injuries in that area, it was thought that the beast was shot and bled on Temo during the attack.

I always like seeing John work; he was a real professional who knew what he was doing. His men weren't slouches, either. However, my main focus right now was covering part of the circle around the workers with my shotgun. This was pretty scary stuff. We knew now that a full point-blank blast of the shotgun could not stop this animal. If lead didn't push him back, silver bullets, even though they may kill him, would not stop his forward momentum.

Just before they were loading the body upon the stretcher, John asked me to give my rendition of what happened during the attack. I said that after Temo fired three shots into the beast, it pounced on him, knocking him to the ground. In order to protect himself, Temo put his left forearm in the beast's mouth to stop it from biting him. During that same period, Temo reached for his pistol and fired two shots, possibly into the animal. The beast then held down his right arm, which held the pistol, and ripped off his left forearm and hand and gave him a bite on the neck. I was standing close to the body while I was pointing these things out to John, then I noticed something very peculiar. There was hair protruding from the victim's lips. I put on some rubber gloves and separated Temo's lips. There was a large tuft of hair in his teeth. He was fighting, biting the wolf back, right to the end.

Everyone around the body just stood there looking in amazement. Here was a guy who stood up to the beast, even though he was overpowered by a superior predator. I had only met him little while ago, but I knew that he went down fighting all the way to the end. He was fighting for his family, his son, and himself. There was a certain respect in the group of men standing around the body. A reverence, even. Here was a fallen warrior, a man of action. He could have played it safe and stayed home, but he decided to follow his own conviction and heart and go at it on his own. Some might call him a stupid man. I prefer to call him a brave man with conviction.

John had us place the dead dog in a plastic bag and rested it on its master's body. As we carried them out of the woods, we move just as slowly and cautiously as we had entering the woods. After this, John didn't have to give orders for us to stay together. Everyone was quiet, alert, and attentive. We stayed very close together. I don't know about the others, but I had a certain feeling of excitement and even accomplishment. It looks like the beast was wounded and bleeding. Temo had proved that. Of course, it has to be confirmed in the lab. But now he's wounded, and he may start making mistakes. I really thought we were on the offensive here. It's a lot easier to trail a wounded animal, and I looked forward to the excitement of the hunt in the morning. I did not, however, look forward to the telling of Temos wife about his demise.

When we got back to Mrs. Ungarini's house, she was waiting in the backyard. She knew we were carrying her husband's body and she just stood there crying into her apron as we passed by. The sheriff and his deputy went over to her and tried to comfort her in this terrible tragedy. She had lost her son and her husband on the same day.

John directed at us to load the body in the mobile lab where we could start working on it. Ultimately, the body and the two surviving dogs would end up at the main laboratory. We had never had any surviving animals that have been attacked and there were many questions that had to be answered. Until that time, the dogs would be quarantined and considered contaminated and infectious.

Five of the men already had dressed into their dissecting laboratory uniform. It was your basic laboratory coat and pants completely covered by an anti-infectious plastic suit. They took the body off the stretcher and laid it down on the dissecting table of the mobile lab. I could have assisted but I didn't want to see any more of Temo in this condition. I felt I should go and say a few words to Mrs. Ungarini. As I was walking toward where she and the sheriff were sitting, John called me over to tell the sheriff that he needed to see him about some very important circumstances concerning this investigation.

I walked back toward the sheriff and Mrs. Ungarini who were both sitting on the back porch. They both looked up at me as I walked over, as if I had some important information to deliver. I slowed down my pace as I got close to them. I went directly to Mrs.

Ungarini and put my hand on her shoulder and said, "I'm so sorry for your loss and for everything that happened to you today. I promise you, we are on the trail of this killer and we won't stop until we get him." She shook her head as if she understood. I quickly turned to the chief and said, "John needs to talk to you about some important circumstances surrounding this investigation." Then I slowly left.

As I was walking away, I glanced back and noticed that the chief was not far behind me. I guess he thought he had done all he could do with the widow. About the time that I reached John in the mobile control Suburban, the chief had caught up to me. John motioned to both of us to have a seat on a couple of chairs in his office. He was on the phone, as usual, planning the next steps of our investigation. I had learned a while ago that he has hundreds of people who he can use working under him. Our program has had authority over every one and every government department that we've been in contact with.

John finally put the phone down and looked at the sheriff and said, "The thing that we are pursuing here is one scary creature. We call it the perpetrator so as not to cause a public panic. It is important that Mrs. Ungarini does not stay at her house for some time. This killer is still lurking in the woods. I don't want her back at the house until we are sure that it has moved on. There will be a tracking party tomorrow morning with specially-trained dogs. They will be able to tell us if he is still around. In the meantime, she should be guarded day and night until we have decided she is no longer in danger. You and your deputies or whoever is guarding her will be issued special silver bullets for your weapons."

The chief looked at John and said, "Are we talking werewolf here?"

John said, "We don't know what it is. It has only been recently that anyone has seen it and survived. We want to make sure that we are covering all bets, so we are issuing silver bullets, just in case."

The chief shook his head yes and said, "I understand."

John turned to me and said, "Make sure all their weapons are loaded with silver bullets before they leave tonight. Make sure they have an ample supply for everyone that may be involved in this operation."

I said "Yes, sir," and took the chief and his deputy over to the supply Suburban.

Just as everything was winding down for the evening at that location, John called me over with some startling news. The agents that had been infected and were thought to be living with their affliction had died. He said he didn't want to go into the details of their deaths, but he thought it would be advisable to talk to June about why they did not survive. So, instead of going on the hunt in the morning, we would be flying in a helicopter to where June was housed. John also said he didn't think the hunt would be too informative. The perpetrator probably accomplished everything he wanted to do with the boy and Temo. Knowing what he knows of him, John said he didn't think it would go after a poor defenseless widow. Even so, we still have to make sure she is protected.

The tracking dogs arrived early in the morning. They were five dogs, four handlers, and seven more agents dressed in combat gear. They left right away and had no trouble picking up the trail. As a matter of fact, they said there were many trails all around the house. Apparently, the creature had been scouting the area for some time. They kept John informed about their progress by handheld radios.

Eventually, they said the one they were following just took a path all in a straight line covering a lot of territory. It was a straight trail; he was not trying to lose anyone. He was just covering a lot of ground and he was moving fast.

The reports remained like that until we left around 10:00 a.m.

This was very informative and left the speculation in my mind that the victims were being handpicked for some reason. When I thought about June's father, he, like Dino's father went up against the beast, they didn't back down; they went to protect their families. Could it be that this beast was selecting men who will defend their family even at the expense of their own lives? Men who would fight to the death to protect their families. And for what reason that he selects such individuals, sport? He wants a prey that fights back. He's a sportsman. He hunts us like we hunt our game.

But how does he know who will stand and who won't? Is this a personality trait or more genetics? I discussed my feelings with John, and he said, "We have a lot to talk to June about."

We were in the helicopter flying to where June was institutionalized. John said there was a lot of construction going on in June's quarters. They were adding additional space and reinforcing the old construction. Apparently, they had decided to keep her there under tighter security with a lot more space. I asked John what was so important that we had to discuss with June, and he said he didn't have time for a discussion at present. He appeared to be busy arranging for kennels and treatment of Temo's injured dogs and what to do with two dead agents' bodies. From what I was hearing from John's conversations, everything was on hold until we talked to June.

The helicopter set down at the prison, and we made our way through all the security checkpoints. John was right about the construction. There were supplies, tools, and equipment up and down all halls, as well as a slight layer of dust from all the construction work. When arriving in June's apartment, we notice that all of the bulletproof glass has been reinforced with large iron rods set in the concrete. An elephant couldn't break out of June's space or break in for that matter.

June was waiting for us in her living room, and we decided to go to the same interviewing room we had talked at before. This time, John took control of the meeting. He explained to June about the two agents who had been attacked and what had happened to them. It seems that their transformation was very much unlike what June went through. During the time of the full moon, they would experience startling changes and transformations, always in great pain and stress. Sometimes the transformations are only partial, especially in the beginning. Later on, when the transformations were more complete, the amount of pain and stress had increased so much that it had finally killed them. They had only lasted three months.

John further explained that at first it was thought that the men could live normal lives for twenty-three or twenty-four days of the month. They had healed remarkably well and were starting to be used doing work in the laboratory. But then it was learned that the transformations had taken so much out of them that in the end they couldn't even get out of bed. It seemed the more complete the transformation the more they suffered until they finally died—part human and part beast.

This was so much unlike June's transformations. It was seven or eight months before one could say she totally transformed. And, although there seem to be some stress and discomfort initially, within a couple of months that had seemed to pass. Also, June had transformed into a smarter and stronger human being.

John looked very seriously at June and asked if she could give us any explanation for what was going on with the two agents who had been attacked and why it was so different from her situation since both were attacked by the same beast.

June looked at us and smiled. She said that although they were all attacked by the same individual, the injuries were extremely different. In her attack, she had received a claw mark to her back which contained very little contamination from the beast, as you called it. The two agents, on the other hand, were bitten several times. The bites were very severe and deep. They also had deep claw marks.

This was a very severe contamination of his DNA. Their bodies could not withstand the onslaught of the very foreign and reactive genetic material with which they were inoculated. Then she looked at us again and said, "You are aware he did this on purpose to these men. He knew they were doomed to die severe and terrible deaths."

Then it occurred to me how contrived and planned that attack had been on the two agents. He knew he was killing them, but he did it on his own timeline.

John just kind of looked down at the floor and shook his head. It was like he just realized the extent to which we were being manipulated. We were on a mission to help these agents to survive and live somewhat normal and productive lives. The beast, on the other hand, knew this was not going to happen. He probably watched the bureau go through all the planning and the expanding of large amounts of energy and money to help these men. He kept us busy and occupied while he searched out other prey.

John gained his composure once again and asked, "Is there a selection process in selecting his victims?"

June nodded her head and said, "Yes, he is very selective."

"This is something we had suspected." Then John quickly came back with, "how does he select and for what reason?"

June smiled again and said, "His senses are far beyond what you could even imagine. As humans, you have to have to discourse, talk to someone for hours to get a sense of who they are. He needs only to see you and get a whiff of you to know more about you than you know about yourselves. He can see your life force and the spiritual aura which surrounds you. Your odor will tell him if you're diseased, your general health, your emotional tone, and how strong a person you are. It's kind of like two dogs meeting, and the first thing they do is to smell each other. They learn more about each other in two seconds than humans would in two hours."

John then said, "Are you able to do this, also?"

June said, "Yes, but not to the extent he is able. At least, not yet."

John said, "What's holding you back?"

June said, "Oh! It's just that he is older and more mature. He's been doing this kind of thing for a very long time and he has sharpened and refined his senses."

All of a sudden, I felt naked in front of June. She was seeing me more completely than I will probably ever see myself. I looked at John and he looked at me and we had no words for each other. I did have one question, but I was too embarrassed to ask. And that was "What are you seeing and sensing in me?"

June didn't give me much time to think because she said, "Gentlemen, I see that you are startled by what I have told you. I did not mean to startle you. I only wanted to tell you the truth about the superior predator you are seeking. And now that the second part of the question you were asking—his reasons. I'm sure he has many reasons and some of them probably overlap. He is definitely a planner who has worked out your every move to each of his. This isn't one who is impulsive. In fact, his mind is too quick for him to be impulsive. He's playing a game, and the object of any game is to win. I have no idea what he's trying to win. I don't think it's as simple as him leading you around to prove to you how superior he is. He could kill hundreds, if he wants, and set this whole country into an uproar that it would take twenty years to calm down. He could make many more like himself, and then mankind would know that they are not at the top of the food chain anymore. He could also communicate with you and lead you to a better existence, but I think this is very far from what he is about. He is definitely playing the role of a superior yet solitary and unknown predator."

June paused a while, took a deep breath, and pensively said, "I think he really dislikes humans. Having been one once himself, he probably remembers the blissful pretending that you know what's going on in your life and in the world when you really don't have a clue. Now, as the most informed creature on this planet, he sees all the futility of the human race, the vanity and self-absorption that you all reek of, and you're his prey. I think he seeks the most challenging victims. He has been doing this for some time, and I think it's probably getting bored. Perhaps he seeking out the best of the best. This is speculation on my part, but I presume you are the best hunters that this country could muster for this job. This might be why he is playing with you."

Then John spoke and something came out of him that I had never heard before. He said, "June, I've been doing this for some time, and if there was anybody better out there, I would give them the job. You know, I don't hate your kind, and perhaps I'm a little envious of your talents. I would not have been on the trail of this perpetrator if he didn't start killing people first. He took people's lives in savage and cruel ways. He fed upon our young. He has been leading us on and on, on purpose. I wouldn't be here, none of us would be here if it wasn't for him. He started this. If this is what he wants, now we have to pursue him no matter what to try to put it to an end whatever it is he is doing."

June looked up with a curious look and asked, "What do you mean when you said he feeds on the young?"

Right then, I realized that she had not been told about her sister in the cabin.

John looked at me, slightly shaking his head back and forth, and said, "Whenever he killed a young child, it appears that he fed on parts of them."

June said, "Did that include my sister?"

John said, "Yes."

June asked, "Did he eat any particular part?"

John said, "Every time, he ate the back muscles."

June reiterated, "I guess he does have a taste for humans, but why does he leave the trail? He is clever enough to cover his tracks. And why did he leave me?"

John said, "We didn't tell you about your sister because we thought it was something that you did not need to know, like the condition of your parents."

June said, "I can understand that but it does not bother me the way you think it would. Please give me all the information you have because it will better help me help you to catch him."

Then John said, "If that's the case, I will have the files of the last three or four attacks sent to you so you can review them."

June said, "Thank you?" Then smiling, June looked up and said, "You have any more questions for me?"

John and I looked at each other and said, "No," this should do it for today. I said that it was nice seeing her again, and I shook her hand. John said goodbye, waved, and walked out of the room. I followed him, taking one last look back at June. She was becoming a very beautiful young woman.

On the way out of the facility, John and I talked about how amazed we are with every meeting with June. I commented that she has so much insight into the human condition. John said, "Yes, she does, but what I'm worried about is the insight she has about us that she's not telling us."

The helicopter was waiting for us, and it wasn't long before we were in the air. John immediately called his superiors and workers.

He told them that the bodies of the two agents, the two dogs, and dog that was alive were all extremely contagious. In order to stop the contagion from spreading, the live dogs had to be put down. Then all of the remains had to be placed in their own secure airtight containers. They were all to be stored at an underground facility where extremely toxic and radioactive chemicals are stored. He gave all these orders with a sense of emergency. I think he just realized how deadly and contagious the remains of the victims could be.

Then he turned to me after all the security measures were in place and said, "I want you to plan to do autopsies on both men and the animals. I want to know what physiologic changes, if any, have taken place in their bodies before and after they died."

I shook my head okay and told him I would probably need a level four or five containment facility to do the autopsies. He said he would email me a list of the facilities, and it would be up to me to pick the one where I can get this done as quickly as possible. I agreed and sat back to rest since it look like things were winding down. We had been hit by one thing after another in the past several months and it was hard to make sense of everything that was happening. I was happy to get a little break, but this did not last for long.

It was near the end of the flight that we received word of another incident. There was another attack but not upon a human, as far as they knew. A large tiger had been killed in its own caged compound. What was so curious and had raised a red flag concerning this report was that there was no evidence of anyone or anything braking in or climbing into the compound. But there was a lot of evidence that there was a serious fight which took place in the compound between the tiger and something else. The tiger did not fare well as it was found beaten, torn, and in pieces.

John immediately had his men send word to the authorities that we would be taking control of the investigation, at least initially. There were agents stationed fairly close the zoo which was in Philadelphia. John ordered them in to take control of the area immediately. Since where we were now was about 600 miles away, we decided to fly and as soon as possible. It would take the mobile lab and rest of the convoy a day to drive in. John thought, and I agreed, that this was a very suspicious criminal occurrence which needed our investigation. It wasn't until we arrived at the scene that we were certain that this was our same ongoing investigation.

Upon arriving at the zoo this morning, our men led us to the tiger's compound. It had been specially prepared for the tiger which was caught in the wild less than a month ago. The tiger was huge, over 800 pounds, and ferocious. He had just come from a life of having to kill in order to eat. This was the draw for the public—a tiger fresh out of the wild. The biggest tiger in captivity. It was billed in the papers and the Internet as being the most dangerous and powerful predator, and pound for pound more powerful than any other creature in the world. Then two weeks into its showing at the zoo, it is found torn apart by something presumably stronger and faster. All the caretakers and their supervisors were walking around, still shaking their heads and wondering what had happened here. It was very clear to us, though, what our perpetrator was saying, "There is no comparison to me. As far as you can see, I'm the best, most ferocious, and most powerful of all killers!"

As we looked around the tiger's compound, it consisted of a den, rocks, a large sandy beach with some plants, and a twenty-seven-foot wide molt which ended in a fifteen-foot wall going straight up. At the top of the wall was a four-foot fence separated by a five-foot iron fence which separated the viewers from the edge of the moat. The moat was filled with water. It was estimated to be eight feet deep where the water met the wall. It was calculated that the tiger would have to jump thirty feet out and over twenty-five feet high to get to the fence if he wanted to try to get out. It was the zoo's opinion that this was twice as much distance and height as he would be able to do.

The zoo was open for business, but they had sealed off the area and erected blinds so no one could look into the tiger's den. We went in through the rear where the attendants usually feed and administer to the animal. The caretaker immediately walked over and pointed out where the tiger was lying. It was upside down on one of the larger rocks about five feet off the ground. His front limb and paw had been

detached at his shoulder and was on the other side of the compound. He had sustained many bite marks on his neck and shoulders. There were deep claw marks on his sides and back. In some places, his ribs were showing because his skin was torn out. Its jaw had been dislocated and detached from one side, yet still hanging from the other. There was hair in his claws and around his teeth where he had torn it out of his opponent. It was that same dark brown hair that we had seen before. Since there was little blood on the rock, we presumed he had been lifted and thrown up there.

The beach area was all torn up, with deep gouges of two kinds of footprints—the tiger's and a large canine-type that was very familiar to us. There was blood and hair spread twenty-five feet in both directions along the beach area. It looked like it had been one heck of a fight, with both combatants really getting into it. I walked over to a piece of tiger skin with fur attached. It was eight inches long and about six inches wide. It had been ripped off during the fight. I noticed it also included the *paniculus carnosis*—a muscle under the skin which humans do not have—thereby making it about two inches thick. I couldn't imagine the amount of force it would take to pull this off a fighting tiger. Such an animal is so tough and physically strong that you could break a baseball bat over their head and you wouldn't even slow it down.

Then I went over to take a look at the tiger's severed limb. It had been pulled out of the shoulder joint, with many of the shoulder tendons still attached. The humerous, or upper limb, was also fractured. Whenever this happened during the fight, it would have left the tiger in a very defenseless position. It appears that's the way it went, since most of the bite marks to the neck were on the same side as the limb separation.

John got his men busy taking blood, hair bite, and saliva samples. He wanted plaster imprints made of the canine footprints. He also stressed that he wanted a lot of photographs of the area, including the positioning of the body of the tiger, because he felt this killing was done in order to make a statement. Then he quickly told the caretaker, his supervisor, and the zoo manager who were standing by that nothing should be said about this incident. As far as anyone should know, the tiger injured itself so severely trying to get out that it died of his injuries. They all looked a little puzzled at the requests and looked at each other, as they shook their heads yes in agreement.

The manager and supervisor quickly left the area. The caretaker, whose name I learned later was John, came up to me and asked me a question. He asked if I had ever seen anything like this before. Without saying anything, I shook my head yes. He then asked, "What would do this kind of thing?"

I told John I didn't really know, no one has really ever seen it, but I thought it would be a good idea if he didn't hang around this area for a while since there is the possibility it might come back.

With that, he looked at me a little scared and said, "You know, there's something else that's strange." He told me that there was animal defecation in the den of the tiger. He told me that tigers never go to the bathroom in their den area; they are very sanitary animals. He showed me where the poo was. It was right in the very spot where the big cat would lie down to rest. I thanked him, and he left. I told John about it, and he immediately had his men take samples. Both John and I agreed that it looked like he was really making a statement with this killing. I wondered if he pooped before or after he dealt with the tiger.

While I was helping with the taking of the hair and saliva samples, the police chief showed up and started asking questions. He wanted to know why the federal government was taking over this case. He had some concerns that the media might get a hold of this and attributed it to UFOs, aliens, and that sort of thing. He also suggested that his detective should be part of the investigations since they know the territory. John assured him that this was an isolated incident from a perpetrator that we have been following for some time. He said the killer is long gone and probably did this only for a shock effect. He said it would be in the public's best interest if we continued with the story that the cat injured itself trying to get out on its pen. That should satisfy the public. The chief said he was sure the public would be satisfied with that story, but he really wasn't.

After all, this had occurred in his jurisdiction, and he thought it was very strange a big cat like that being killed in his own enclosure. He also said that we were hiding something from him. John agreed that this was a very strange occurrence and that at this point in the investigation it would not be productive to share all of our information with the local authorities. He said that, as a professional, he was sure the chief could understand his position. The chief looked like he knew he was politely being blown off. He shook his head yes and walked away over to some of his men who were guarding the enclosure. John looked at me and smiled, and I smiled back.

That policeman had no idea of what he wanted to get involved in, and he was so much better off by not knowing.

The forensics were just about complete, and I had to schedule to do the autopsies. I had ambivalent feelings about doing the autopsies. I was a little frightened about the contamination aspect of working with the bodies and would also be very interested in what I might find. I thought it was quite a privilege since I was one of the few people in the United States to dissect and do an autopsy on a werewolf.

I picked out a level five hospital to conduct the autopsies. It was within 300 miles. I had to go through different catalogs and computer stores to order and make sure all the equipment would be at the hospital on time. The CDC had a lot of what I was looking for.

The hospital and vendors were notified by John and his assistants that I would be there in the next couple of days to receive the equipment, bodies, and animal carcasses. I decided to take some time off by driving to the location and holding up in a hotel. I thought I would get a day or so off, but people kept calling me about what specific type of equipment I would need and how many assistants would be there. I had to discuss and fine tune everything on the list for just about everything I needed. They wanted to be very efficient in supplying all the equipment. They wanted to know what type of table I wanted, not just what it should look like but the model and make. I had to pick it out of the catalogs they emailed me, as well as the type of gowns, gloves, face protection equipment, and selecting from a whole array of microscopes, slides, and x-ray equipment. I told them initially it would just be me, dictating equipment and a couple of level five assistances to help me with the dissection and moving the bodies around during the weighing and disposing of the remains. And these individuals had to have special clearance with John and his group. I had no idea they would go into such detail, and it seemed like the easiest part of this operation was procuring the level five assistants. However, I was glad I did the extra work because I got everything I would need and some things I probably wouldn't need, but they were just for backup. It seemed like this was not only a level five operation but also a level one priority.

Morning came too quickly when I had to be at the at the autopsy room at seven a.m. The bodies were already there, and the assistants were waiting for me outside the door. There were the usual armed guards stationed at the door; there were four of them and a couple of men in black suits. One of the men in suits introduced himself and checked our IDs. He wanted to make sure that we were familiar with the level five protocol. He said upon entering the rooms we would see a dressing room with protective suits and gear, a decontamination room for when we finished the autopsies or if there was an accident, and finally the autopsy room which was outfitted with everything that we had asked for and anything else they could think of that we might need.

We shook our heads yes and agreed with the gentleman and went into the first room. I thought it was important to verbally prepare them before we went into the lab. I quickly learned from them that they were not briefed on who we were going to autopsy and the type of autopsy we would be doing. They were only told that this was top-secret and that whatever went on in the lab could not be discussed with anyone. I told them we would be autopsying two human beings and three dogs. I told them because there was a possibility of contagion, known only at this time to occur by breaks in the skin, we were not going to take a chance and we would double protect and double glove ourselves. They agreed.

We started with both the agents who had recently died. Uncovering their bodies out of the sealed containers, I discovered creatures that were half man, half beast. They were partially covered with hair in patches around their bodies. It was about an inch and a half long and it came out of a tough canine skin. The other parts of their body appeared to be human, although it did not have a totally human texture. Their faces were tortured and showed they died in extreme pain. One had canine teeth and a snout, and the other had five-inch canine ears projecting from its hairy skull. Immediately, the two men stood back and started saying things like "Is this real?" and "I don't believe this." I could see the two assistants, who were with me, were stunned and frightened. I stepped back and told both of these men working with me that these were real people who had been infected and how I understood their total surprise and how shocking this was to them because when I first learned of this, it was just as shocking to me. I reassured them this was top-secret, and they could not discuss this with anyone. I also said that with protective clothing we would be safe from any contamination. They said they understood but still looked shaky as we proceeded.

Incisions were made into both of the bodies. These were the classic Y-shaped cuts that are done in human autopsies. Their skin was tough and animallike. It was very thick. It was so thick and hard to get through that I thought we should weigh the bodies before continuing. These men were about five feet ten and six feet tall and weighed 255 lbs. and 280 lbs. They were much heavier than they appeared. They should have been about 175 and 195.

With this information, I knew that we should be looking for something that was giving the extra weight to these men. I had been doing this work for some time and by sight had underestimated their weight by eighty or ninety pounds.

Their skin looked like typical canine skin. Inside was the *paniculus carnosis*, the muscle tissue found within animal skin. The whole skin was infiltrated by small tumorlike masses about three-eighths of an inch in diameter.

As I cut into the torsos, I noticed all the tissues were infiltrated with these hard tumorlike structures. They were whiteish and about an inch in diameter. They were found all through all parts of the skin and in the organs. They looked like a gumma type of tissue that you find in syphilis. They were bumpy and swollen and had an extensive blood supply. Some of them had hair and hide exuding from them; those were the ones near the surface of the skin. We excised many of them and weighed them. They were a very heavy tissue for their size. These gumma were probably the contributing factor in the men's excessive weight.

They also appeared to be instrumental in the transformation between man and beast and man again. We found different types of tissues exuding from them. In the skin, it was hair. Near the bones, it was bone. And near the organs and brain, it was organ and brain tissue.

We removed and weighed all the organs. They were all more heavy than they appeared. They were all infiltrated with these gumma-type of structures. It was most interesting when we discovered that the organs most infiltrated with these structures was the brain and nervous system. I thought to myself these might account for June's increased intellectual abilities and increased strength.

We repacked the bodies in the containers and included all the equipment coverings and gloves—anything that had been in contact with them. The only thing we did not repacked were samples of the tumorlike structures that we had discovered. I wanted to do microscope evaluations to try to classify what type of tissue this was. The DNA of the samples are needed to be compared with human DNA and observed under an electron microscope and any other way our geneticists would see fit to evaluate and determine its origin.

The autopsy of the two dogs who had been killed went quickly. There were no changes to be seen, and it appeared they had died of their wounds. We took a few slides and looked the tissues in the microscope to make sure. Just to be safe, we took a few samples for the histology and for the geneticists to view. The remains of the last dog who had stayed alive for some time told a different story.

There were minute little gummalike tumors throughout its body. The dog's weight was not much more than we had expected. There was no concentration of the tumors in any areas. These findings really causes me to ask some question as to whether the infection operates differently in a canine or if it did not have enough time to organize itself and grow. We took some more samples of these tumors.

They didn't appear any different from the tumors or gumma that we had taken from the humans. We resealed the animals in their specific containers. It was late, around 9:00 p.m., and we were all tired. We decontaminated our uniforms and ourselves and left. The guards were still outside, and they looked as exhausted as we were. They asked if we were finished and if they could have the containers removed to their storage area. I told them yes and that there were samples that had to be sent to our laboratory at the CDC. Just then, another gentleman stepped forward and identified himself as the supervisor and preserver of the remains. He said that he had been watching the autopsy by video camera. He said he would make sure that the samples were put in special containers and transported to the proper laboratories. He wanted to make sure that there were no accidents known or unknown.

He needed to make sure no one was contaminated by the remains that were in the lab. He said it was our duty to come forward and tell him because of the seriousness of this investigation. He then said he wanted to take, as part of his procedure, both nasal and buccal swabs of all participants in the autopsies. He also wanted to take samples from our faces and hands. I guess he didn't trust the fact that we had double protected ourselves with two layers of protective clothing, as well as double gloving our hands and arms. We also had on respirators covering our faces under the protective suits. Well, everybody had to do their job. Though I have to admit that it was a surprise to me that we were being videotaped.

I had to eat, so I went to the closest restaurant. On the way over, John called me and said he had heard that I had completed the autopsies. He asked if I had made any discoveries, and I told him about the gumma and that we needed a lot more investigation as to what they were and how they were operational in this disease. He told me that we had another lead surface and that he wanted to discuss it with me in the office. I said that I would leave in the morning as soon as possible. It seems things were not slowing down at all.

I was able to get to John's office about midday the next day. He said that he had reviewed my results of the autopsy and that he was glad I took so many samples because we were going to need a lot of investigation into the gumma-looking tumors. He also related that he had called several expert histologists to evaluate the tissues. I agreed with him that this was probably the next step since we were dealing with something we've never seen before. I told him that I would be looking very anxiously to see their report. He also said that he had lined up the use of an electron microscope for the histologists. I shook my head, agreeing with him that was a good step, also.

I think the discussion on the autopsy had pretty much ended and I asked him what other developments had occurred. John said that there had been a werewolf sighting in the New Orleans area. It had been covered in several of the local newspapers. What made the report so interesting was that it was made by a teacher who was taking a mid-evening stroll. The newspapers have downplayed the sighting by suggesting that the teacher was in some way mistaken. Convincingly enough, she had stuck by her story, even though she had received a lot of backlash from doing so.

John wanted me to go down and interview the lady, talk to the local police, and investigate the area where the sighting had occurred. He already booked the flight down to New Orleans for me. I was leaving later that evening, flying into Baton Rouge. He said he was sure I could handle this investigation on my own, but if I get any indication that it's our predator, to let him know immediately. He handled me a special pass to allow me to carry my firearms in my luggage. He reminded me to never go out without my firearm. I said, "Don't worry. After what I've seen, you won't catch me running around naked." I said bye and left to pack.

It was a three-hour flight down and I arrived too late at night to make an appointment with the teacher who had seen some animal. I got a good night sleep and called her early the next morning. She said she can see me after work, around six o'clock. I told her I was a government investigator who specializes in these types of sightings. She was surprised that someone from the federal government would be interested in hearing about her experience. I told her that my particular department likes to follow these things up and that I'd see her at six o'clock at her house.

I arrived about fifteen minutes before the meeting. Her name was Ms. Stanton and she was a local high school teacher. When I knocked at the door, it was opened by an attractive forty-five-year-old woman who was very businesslike and handled herself very professionally. In the small talk before I asked her exactly what had happened, she related to me that she taught History and English at the high school. She had hoped to teach special needs students but the only openings locally were in English and History. So, before she could teach, she had to become certified in both of the classes. She had been at the school about three years and totally enjoyed her work. I noticed there were a lot of running pictures of her and what looked like students. She said that she was an avid runner who try to do at least fifteen miles a week. She said she was also the coach of the girls track team at the high school. I congratulated her because I knew that running was a very demanding sport. She immediately got right into how the sighting had occurred. She related that since the track season was over she had a little more time on her hands in the evenings. On this particular night, about eight o'clock, she decided to take a walk on a path along one of the many canals in the area. Since she lived in a rural area, there weren't many houses around. She had taken this walk many times down the path by the canal about two miles to the Cajun community where the canal empties into the river. She said she always carried a flashlight because you never knew when you might step on a water moccasin or some other type of poisonous snake. There was nothing else to really be frightened of since she knew many of the students and their parents at the Cajun community. It seems, because the Cajun community is bilingual, they are always a little weaker in English. She said that many times she had to tutor the Cajun students and give them extra help for which they were very grateful.

Anyway, she was about a quarter of a mile from the river. It was nighttime, and she was briskly walking with the light focused about five or six feet in front of her. It was a warm night and the snakes would be out, so she was concentrating on the lighted path before her. All of a sudden, she heard something like a growl and a sound or something like a thump about forty or so feet away. She immediately aimed the beam of her light in that direction and saw something that was hard to believe. There was a bipedal animal seven feet or more tall standing next to a chair and holding something. It looks straight at her and she could see its red eyes glaring at her. It turned and ran off the path away from the canal and into the woods, holding what look like a small person. The whole occurrence was probably less than two seconds. She had never seen anything so large move so fast. She said the body was as big as a cow or small horse. It was covered in dark brown fur. She immediately turned and ran back home. On the way home, she called 911 on her cell phone and reported the incident to the police. They said that they would send the sheriff out to investigate. They called her back a couple of hours later and told her they didn't see anything. She thought the incident was over. The local newspaper picked up the report and published the incident in the paper. For a couple of weeks, she received a lot of calls kidding about what happened. Since there are no Bigfoot sightings in the area, the paper attributed to a loup-garou or werewolf sightings. I asked her if she had ever again walked the canal. She says that she still walks it but only in the daytime. She says she's afraid to go at night.

I asked her if she would show me the spot where all this took place and she agreed, but it would have to be a couple of days later on Saturday. We agreed to meet at her house at ten o'clock and drive to and park at the Cajun community and walk down to the area. I said goodbye and left. This would give me a couple of days to talk to the local police.

On the way back to my hotel room, I received an urgent text from my wife. It said that I should call her as soon as possible because she had to discuss some important issues. I felt I was hot on the trail once again and I didn't feel like getting involved in my wife's issues, but I'd called her when I got back to the room.

My wife quickly picked up the phone with only one ring and told me it was about time I got back to her. She immediately went into her tirade about how this had been long enough and how the family felt that I had deserted them by making this investigation more important than their needs. She said it was important that I come home now and leave this part science fiction and part pipe-dream pursuit of mine if I valued our relationship at all. I explained that I was down to New Orleans in the middle of a specific assignment and that I would be back just as soon as it was over, not more than a week. She started to accuse me still putting the project before the family and of disengaging from all feelings that I had had of our relationship and marriage. I assured her that was not the case and that the call had come at a bad time. If she had called three or four days before, I would have declined the assignment. Now it would be desertion in the field. I told her I hope that she understood that I just could be in the middle of something so important. Finally, she said, "Well, I see your position hasn't changed at all and you still are continuing to fail to take any responsibility for our relationship or your family." She said "Goodbye, Jordan," and hanged up.

I knew she sounded mad, but I also knew she did not know how important this investigation was. I was hoping to track down a killer. Even more important to me was the fact that even though I was a physician, this is the first time I was actually helping to save lives. I felt something calling me from inside, and the impetus to continue on to fulfill myself and my destiny. And people and the government were counting on me. I had to go on.

The next call I made was to the police chief of the particular parish where the sighting occurred. I asked the chief if I could come in and talk to him and the officers that followed up on the report. He said that he didn't mind my coming in. However, he thought it would be a waste of time since his officers didn't turn up anything. He said these types of sightings occur occasionally, but with investigation, they never really pan out with any type of realistic evidence. I made an appointment to see him next day around 10:00 a.m. and asked that the officers would also be available, and he said he would make them come in by that time.

I arrived a little early for the appointment. I was surprised to see the police station so busy that morning. I wondered why it was all abuzz. I found that very quickly when I showed up at the front entrance and a reporter from the local newspaper thrust a tape recorder in front of my face, asking what information I had about the werewolf sighting. I told him I didn't have any information yet since I had not discussed the incident with the police. The reporter was persistent and asked if I was the government's official werewolf hunter. I said, "Oh no! This is just part of Homeland Security, and we want to make sure no one is causing a threat to anyone else." As I made my way in, a couple of officers were at the door to make sure the reporter and his entourage didn't follow me into the station.

It was a small police station—a fifteen by twenty-five feet reception area with chairs and a counter with three desks behind. There were two offices behind them and a couple of cells for lockup. The chief was standing in front of his office and waved for me to come over. He asked me to take a seat in front of his desk. He was all smiles and in an apparently happy mood. The first words out of his mouth after I had taken a seat were, "You're big news around here. It's hard to keep a secret in a small town where everyone knows everyone else. I'm sorry for all the publicity. I didn't mean for this to happen."

I assured him that I understood and said that their presence shouldn't have any impact upon what we discussed here. I also said that all the information that we discussed should be considered confidential and was not for public knowledge. I asked him to describe the report and the investigation that followed in the sighting of some creature. He opened the file folder and said they received a report about nine 9:30 p.m. from woman who said she had seen a large bipedal animal who looked to be carrying another human being, running off the path by the canal. Officers were dispatched to the area of the reported citing. They searched the area and talked to members of the Cajun community which was nearby. Nothing was found, and no one had seen or heard anything suspicious. I asked the chief if anyone had searched the area during the day, and he said he felt there was no reason to do so. I asked if they had a K-9 dog with the investigating officers, and he said they did not have one at the station and he saw no reason to bring one in. I pause a while and then asked, "Does your station have many of these types of sightings?"

He says that he receives at least one every couple of years. They investigate them but they never turn out anything significant.

Then I made the statement to him that compared to the rest of the country his area has an abnormal amount of werewolf sightings and I asked if he was aware that. He said that he was aware of that fact and that he and his men do investigate every report but they don't turn up anything. I then asked him how he accounts for these sightings in his parish. He said, "Well, we think it's that swamp gas. People go walking along the canal at night, and if the breeze is just right, they can get a load of that green swamp gas. It can get you high and cause hallucinations and all kind of stuff. Heck, those Cajun people living down there breathe it all the time. They're crazy. A breed unto themselves. They kinda keep to themselves. They don't bother us, and we don't bother them. Of course, their kids have to go to school and that's when you may see them. Other than that, they just hang around their own community. They live off the river and any supplies they need they have delivered to their general store."

He went on to say, "It's my understanding that the teacher who made the report made it a habit of tutoring students at the Cajun community. She may have gotten a little more of that gas or have been a little more susceptible to it than most of us people. Not saying that's the exact reason why she saw what she saw, but it is the most reasonable explanation I have at this time. If you really want to find out about werewolves, I would go down to that Cajun community and talk to those people. They've got a lot of old wives' tales. I don't know if it'll be true, but I do know it will be very colorful and interesting."

I thank him very much for the information. I said, "I have one more question for you before I interview the investigating officers. Have you ever seen a werewolf?"

He smiled and said, "No! And I don't ever want to see one."

Then I said, "So you don't go walking down by the canal at night?"

He said, "No, I don't go down there looking for trouble. We're a small community up here and we have enough trouble that finds us here that we don't have to go looking for any more."

I thanked him very much for the interview, and he asked the two other officers to come into his office to talk with me.

The officer said exactly what was on the report. They were told to investigate an animal sighting. They searched the path about one hundred yards in either direction of the area in question. They saw no blood, no footprints, no chair, no animals. They did say there was a lot of that swamp gas coming off the canal that evening.

They interviewed several people at the Cajun community, and no one said they had heard or seen anything. I asked them if they had ever seen a werewolf or knew anyone personally that had seen one. They said that they had never seen one and that they knew of no one personally that had seen one. However, being on the force, they occasionally have the opportunity to interview someone who says they had seen one. One of the officers did volunteer that in this last sighting the woman—a teacher—was considered a very reputable person and that her report was one of the most exacting and complete report that they had taken of such an occurrence. I thanked them very much for the time and told the chief that I was going to leave. He had the desk clerk see me out of the office right to the reporter who was still waiting for me.

The reporter started asking if I had any additional information, and I told him, "No. No additional information or evidence." I quickly jumped in my car and left.

Saturday came very quickly for my meeting with Ms. Stanton at the Cajun community. It was nice to get a couple of quiet days after all the commotion at the sheriff's office. I felt rested and felt excited to see the location where the sighting had occurred. Just before I left Ms. Stanton called me and told me she would meet me at the Cajun community because she had a few important errands to run in the morning. I really didn't mind because it would give me some more alone time.

The road into the Cajun community was a dirt road about three and a half miles off the main highway. It was a well-maintained road with the side-lying grass and trees being well trimmed. I was surprised to see an asphalt road starting as I entered the town which consisted of beautiful little quaint homes with sidewalks and gardens all well-kept. The middle of town had streets with asphalt and brick walkways.

There was a large modem general store which looked like it carried everything imaginable. This certainly wasn't what I had expected from the sheriff's description of some gypsy-like isolated people who lived on the river and kept to themselves, with little contact to the outside world. A closer look revealed dishes for television and cable on almost every building. There were no older cars or trucks on the streets; they all were two to three years old. And the most amazing thing was the boats. Since these people were supposed to have lived off the river, I expect to see some old boats tied up to the homes and docks. There were only a lot of new speedboats and party boats. It looked like these folks were doing really well and better than most.

I had gotten there a good half hour before the meeting time so I could look around a little. Everyone on the street quickly noticed that I was a stranger. They were friendly and smiled and went about their own business. I stopped into the general store for cup of coffee. The clerk, who looked like he might be the owner of the establishment mentioned that they don't get many tourists down this way and asked if I needed help with anything. I said I was there for a meeting and wouldn't be staying long. As I left the store, I noticed he was talking to someone on his cell phone.

Ms. Stanton arrived, and I greeted her and asked her if she'd like a cup of coffee. She said she had just had one and would like to get on with showing me where the sighting had occurred. I went to my car and got my camera, and we walked about one hundred yards to a canal where we could see down a long path about ten feet wide going straight along the canal. She said the site was about 250 yards, less than a quarter of a mile down the canal. We walked down, and she stood and planted her feet firmly on the ground and stated, "This is the spot where I saw that thing."

I asked her if I could take a couple of pictures of her pointing to where she had seen the incident for my supervisor so they could get the general lay of the land. She agreed and posed for a few pictures. In one of the pictures, I asked her to point to where she saw the creature exit into the woods. I went and made an X on the ground because I wanted to come back later and search for any evidence. Then we walked back to her car, and I said goodbye.

I hurried back to the area where I placed the X mark on the ground and went into the woods to investigate. It was medium dense brush and mostly loose swamplike vegetation on the ground. It looked like there were people walking around this particular area because there were a lot of tracks leading into the woods and back, but I saw no indicative signs of what I was looking for. I searched for about forty-five minutes in expanding circles and was about one hundred yards out from the canal path and actually very close to the dirt road coming into the community when I saw a footprint. It was that same large caninelike footprints with an indentation in about three inches in the soft soil and mud. It was very curious. I couldn't find any footprints leading up to this area, just this one. Then there were a few more leading toward the dirt road. I took pictures of the footprints and the whole area, as well as pictures leading back to the canal path. In my mind, this verified that we were on the right track and that our wolfman was down here, also.

I walked back to the end of the canal path and into the Cajun village. I noticed there were three men leaning up against my rental car waiting for me. I didn't know if they were going to be trouble. As I walked toward them, I pressed my left elbow against my jacket to make sure my pistol was still in the holster. I knew it was there, but I just had to reassure myself.

As I got close to them, two of the men walked away and one of the men walked toward me, smiling. He was about five foot nine, with dark pants, a blue button shirt, and gold vest. He had long curly black hair, a gold earring, and he looked like a gypsy He said, "Hi boss! How you today? Jou know Ms. Stanton? She is good teacher. She help with kids school. Jou looking for something?"

I just said I asked her to show me something.

He said, "Oh, where she thought she saw a loup-garou?"

I said, "Something like that." Then I asked, "Do you know anything about it?"

Then he got a really strange and serious look and said, "We, Cajun people, keep to ourselves. We don't bother nobody, and we don't want the world to bother us. There is no loupgaroux here." As he said that, he took a good hard look at my camera.

I thanked him and told him I had to be going.

He said, "You have good night, boss. Come back anytime. There nothing dangerous here."

I got in my car and left, thinking that was a nice friendly send-off. I guess he was trying to calm any fears I had. The truth was I had seen and taken pictures of the footprints. And now I knew there was a wolf here.

Morning started early for me. I had to get in touch with John and give him a report of my findings from this investigation. I decided to do all that after a good breakfast. Little did I know that there would be more information forthcoming which would put a whole different spin or viewpoint on what I had discovered. I was just beginning to learn what was going on down here.

When I got back to the motel, I noticed there were five men and two vehicles waiting for me where I usually park my car. The men looked Cajun. One of their vehicles was a new pickup truck with lights on top, sides, on the running boards, and any other place that the buyer may have an option to put them. The other car was a new Lincoln with just as many options, including a hood scoop. It was evident that these cars were worth a lot, and the men stood around them, grinning like forty-year-old adolescents proud of their wheels. None of these men looked familiar to me.

One of the men, who had chrome-tipped boots, walks over to me as I'm getting out of the car. He says, "Hi, boss. We wanted to talk to you, you were not here. I hope you don't mind that we waited."

I said, "I don't mind too much. What do you want to talk about?"

He said, "Can we talk inside?"

I nodded my head yes and also said "Sure."

Almost immediately, he waved off three of the men to stay with the vehicles, and he and the one closest to him started walking with me toward my motel door. I let them in the room and showed them to a table which just happened to have three chairs. They sat, and I followed. Then he started by saying, "Now, boss, you don't believe those old wives' tales that there are loupgaroux?"

What a leading question. I guess he wants to find out what I knew on the subject and, more specifically, if I had found anything else on my investigation in his territory. Well, why not tell him because I know that he knows they exist.

After a little pause, I decided to say, "I suspect there are things in your community that you don't want people to know about. Concerning wolfmen, also known as loupgaroux, I know they exist. I have seen one several times. I have followed his killing path and seen his victims. All were ripped apart and some were eaten, especially the children. And now he's been seen taking a victim near your community. I have seen his footprints down there. I would really like to know why you would try to protect such a creature."

With that statement, he just stared, not at me but through me as if he had become lost in his own mind. Then after a while he slowly turned and looked at his partner and then he looked back at me and said, "Where you see this wolfman?"

I said, "Up near Minnesota, and I have been trailing him for almost a year now."

He shook his head yes and looked at me and said, "This is not that one."

I said, "Could you explain yourself?"

Once again, he said, "This loupgaroux is not the one you have been chasing."

I said, "How do you know?"

And he again said, "Because he never leaves the Cajun compound."

I said, "But, still, why do you protect such a creature?"

Then he began a very heartfelt explanation. "Please, boss, you must understand. This one is not like that one. This loupgaroux has been with the Cajun community for over one hundred years. He helps us, and we protect him. How you think we survive? You think we live off the river like in the old days. The game is gone. The fish are gone. Yet we live good. We have nice homes. We have nice cars and boats. Everything we need we have."

He then took a deep breath and said, "You think we smart enough to do this all on our own? We don't steal. We don't sell drugs. We are honest people. This loupgaroux, he is very smart. He shows us how to invest. He makes millions for our community. Everyone knows and likes him. He just hangs around our community. He likes to fish. He never goes into the town. He is a danger to no one."

"I know the teacher told you what she saw. But she did not know what she saw. You know, Cajun people do not die in hospital. We born in the community and we die in the community. Sometimes, if a person is suffering like the one the teacher saw, they asked to be put out by the canal at the time of the full moon. This

last one was ninety-two years old. She had smoked for seventy years and had emphysema. She could not breathe. She was choking on her own spit. She said she couldn't wait any longer, so we sent her out early that night by the canal."

"Believe me, he moves so fast that they never know what hit them, even though they are expecting it. It is all mercy, and it's lot better than dying in a hospital bed. We did not expect anyone to be on the trail around nine o'clock that night, and he was sent to bless her early. The relatives were supposed to pick up her chair as soon as it was finished. Initially, he thought that the teacher was a relative who had come early to pick up the old woman's chair. Very quickly, though, he realized it was a stranger. Then the reports came in the papers and Internet."

"Investigators and reporters came, and we have to deny everything in order to survive. Wolfman you seek is not here. He is a very bad one. He is up North. He loves to play games with the authorities. He is smarter than you and will lead you wherever he wants. If he comes down here, our loupgaroux will kill him because he is bad. Our loupgaroux is older, smarter, and stronger. He has lived hundreds and hundreds of years. His heart is not like the other one. He wants to be of service to humanity. He has found a place with people who need him.

"You say you have seen that one several times. As far as we know, no one has ever seen him and lived. If you are alive, it is because he has future plans for you. I would be very careful for myself and for my family. He is very clever. You cannot have enough protection. Has anyone else that you know seen him?"

I said, "No one and I understand that even close relatives of people killed who have never been in contact with it been killed, also."

He looked down at the table and said, "This looks very bad that he is leading you run around, hunting for him and talking about him." Then he said, "Please do not report about our friend and provider. He is a danger to no one. Even during the full moon, he may not change because he has that much control. We lock him up in special room three days before and three days after the full moon.

During that time, we sit with him at night so he does not hurt anyone, including himself. If people come down here looking for him, he will go away and we will be left on our own. We cannot make it for long on our own. The Cajun people are good people. We keep to ourselves. We don't hurt no one. We have no crime in our community. The sheriff, even he knows that we cause no problems and that we police ourselves. What the sheriff sees is that he has a community of a couple of hundred people where he has to do no work. He likes to keep it that way, and we like to keep it that way."

After that statement, he looked at me with his dark wanting eyes. I knew he was asking me to help protect the livelihood of his people. In no way had I expected something like this. Especially when I found the footprints, I thought I was really back on my original hunt for the killer I had been tracking. Now this information gave me a whole new dimension into not only what I was hunting but who I was hunting. Even though I was very thankful for the information I had just heard, I realized that I was not on the right trail. The newspaper and Internet reports that I had reviewed had some validity and were informational, but they did not relate to the case I was working on.

I got out of my chair and stood behind it, with my hands resting on the chair back. I told them, "Thank you for letting me know what was really going on down here." I tried to reassure them that I had no interest in their friend and provider and that I thought my boss would not have any interest, either. I told them that I was required to make a complete report of my findings but that anything in the report would never reach the public. That is because we are a top-secret organization which was started with one purpose and that was to track down and stop this killer.

They both got up from their chairs and thanked me, as they shook my hand and left. I was pretty sure that nothing would be done, except a monitoring of any strange occurrences in this area. But now I had to write the report for John. As I thought about it, it seemed that my report would initiate a lot more questions about what was really going on. There were questions about why this Northern wolf was coming out at this time. Was he just bored and wanting to play games with the authorities or did he have a more sinister and evil plan? And most interesting was why I was still around and how did I fit into his machinations.

I had a lot to say but, boy, was it hard getting started. The dictations came very slowly, and I had to rewrite them many times on the computer. I also had to make flight arrangements back to Washington tomorrow. It's going to be a very busy day.

I had finished my work the night before and was packing for my flight at three in the afternoon. It was about 10:30 a.m. when my room phone rang. It was a pleasant-speaking gentleman without a Cajun accent. He addressed me by name and introduced himself. He said he was the Cajun community's friend and provider. He said he was calling me because Victor had talked to him about our meeting and he thought he should touch base with me concerning his feelings about my experiences with the werewolf up North. He said he was doing this for no other reason than it might save my life and the lives of my family. I told him that he was the last person in the world that I thought I would hear from. I related to him that this was amazing and frightening and that he had caught me off guard. He told me to please not be afraid; he was just trying to help.

He said, "The fact that you are alive after seeing him and that he has allowed you to find enough information to follow him reveals that he has plans for you. He is grooming you for an eventual outcome. The fact that he has left a trail indicates he wants to be followed." He then asked, "Are you sure that there are no other individuals who had seen him and lived?"

I said, "Maybe one."

He asked, "Does that person work on the investigation, as well?"

I said, "No, they are being sequestered presently in a safe house."

He asked, "Were they bitten?"

I answered, "Yes!"

He asked, "Is it a female?"

I said, "Yes."

Then he said, "Oh, I see."

He pauses for a while and said, "There is something I have to tell you about werewolves. The only way that a werewolf can make his line stronger is to mate with another werewolf. The offspring in that would be much stronger and smarter than the parents. The young are extremely difficult to raise. This is because of their intellect and strength. They have to be taught how to control themselves, especially at the time of the full moon. Like all adolescents, they resist parental discipline and want to be their own boss. To the best of my knowledge, no one recently has ever raised a baby werewolf to adulthood. It may have been possible 300 or 400 years ago, but now with all the information and technology it gets more and more difficult to hide."

"This female you are hiding, I hope she is very well protected. He has created her, and he knows she exists. He might even know where she is. You know, we can smell our kind up to fifty miles away. I'm sure he has plans for her. I'm just not sure how you fit into the whole picture. But whatever you do, do not tell her what I had just told you. She may try to seek him out. I'm sure at some time he will try to seek her out. You must not let that happen. This wolfman from the North is not strong enough or disciplined enough to raise a baby werewolf."

I then said to him, "Why don't you help us find him?"

He said, "We usually keep to ourselves and don't bother each other. There are not many of us around, and we know each other's scent. If one of us were to go after him, he might do something terrible like infect fifty people a day, cause an epidemic, go to the newspapers and Internet. We would all have to go into hiding, and many people would be hurt. You see, most of us wish to help humanity. Wherever we are, we're trying to help people. We do this without a lot of notoriety so we aren't found out. There are many people who depend upon us, and this bad wolfman could ruin everything that we have been trying to do."

Then he quickly changed the demeanor of his voice and said, "Well, I think I have given you enough information so you will have some idea what this perpetrator has in mind and you will be better able to protect yourself. I hope I have helped you."

I said, "I think you have."

Then he said goodbye and hung up.

I first thought was *Wow!* Now I have a lot more information for the report. My second thought was these creatures are very smart and manipulative. I really wonder what he was trying to accomplish by telling me this. At that point, my head went into a whorl. I couldn't think straight. I was on overload. Entirely too many things and ideas were assaulting my mind at once. I just sat on my bed wondering what just happened.

Later that afternoon when I reached the airport for my flight to Washington I was still in a partial daze. I was rushing around trying to get to the airport on time and had not had a chance to gather my thoughts on what it happened in the morning. I finally started to make some sense of what happened when I was resting in my seat on the airplane. I pulled up my computer and made an addendum to the report for John which included the conversation I had had with the Cajun provider. I liked calling him a Cajun provider because his lifestyle was not like the werewolf we were hunting. I related everything that I was told in the morning conversation except the fact that these werewolves could try to double their strength and intelligence by mating with one another. I thought that would protect June because John might consider her existence and the possibility of her mating as a threat to the whole human race. Since I knew John always dealt with threats upfront, he might decide to sterilize June or eliminate her completely. I did not want to see that happen to such an innocent girl.

The next morning, I walked into John's office and he said that a packet had arrived for me and that he thought I should take a look at. It was a large manila folder addressed to me and care of our office. It wasn't from anyone I knew. It was some law firm's name and address stamped in the corner. I got a really bad feeling as I opened the package. There was a letter on top with several forms stapled together with little sticky notes showing me where to sign. It was a notice; my wife was filing for divorce.

John looked at me and asked if I'd like to have some time off to deal with it. I told him, "It looks like things are pretty well laid out here. I'll deal with it after the meeting later today."

Then John said, "Okay, let's get into your report."

I had emailed the report before I got off the plane. John had already reviewed it and had a list of questions that he had written down on a paper in front of himself. Before he started on the paper, he looked at me and said, "You know, Jordan, since you have been with us, we have compiled more information on this phenomenon than we had collected in my three years as head of the team or even before I even was here. There has also been more activity by this predator while you have been with us. I'm not entirely sure what the full meaning of this is, but I do feel we are getting closer. This may be by our design or it may be by his own plan, but I do believe we are learning more about him and getting closer to him. Now you've discovered another one, and we have two problems to deal with. Even though you picture him as a more philanthropic, supportive, and caring creature, in my mind, he still possesses the ability to pass this curse on to other individuals." He then looked me straight in the face and asked, "How great is the possibility that he might do that?"

I looked at John and said, "I think it's a very low possibility. The Cajun people need him, and they protect him. I don't think things will change down there unless there is a big shakeup in the social structure. From what I got from talking to their wolfman, he enjoys being their godlike provider. He's been there a long time and doesn't appear to have any other aspirations than providing economic support for the people who protect and hide him."

John said, "How well do those people live?"

I told him, "They live well above their own means of support. They live on the river in nice homes with nice cars and boats. They had no reportable crime, no drug addictions, or drug dealers. The sheriff says they tend to police themselves, and he never hears of any problems. You might say, they have a really good thing going there."

John said, "I think you're right about that. I don't want to do anything down there that would negatively impact those people. It is, however, our duty to keep an eye on the situation and from time to time we may have to go down to take a look around to see that the status quo is being maintained." Looking right at me, John said, "I'd like to have you as part of that observation team."

I nodded my head and said, "I do have a little rapport with those people, and I'll be glad to help out as much as I can."

Looking up from his paper, John said, "There seems to be some animosity between this wolfman and the one we are hunting."

I said, "Yes, the New Orleans one is more interested in being of service to mankind and has positioned himself to that effect. The more Northern one we are after seems to enjoy playing ego games to show up the human population as weak and stupid. He tries to give himself a feeling of superiority, although with his kind, he is considered the most inferior. I'm sure that any wolfman out there doesn't like the publicity he is causing. I don't think they care if we get rid of him."

John looked at me and said, "Well, that's what we're trying to do. Oh, by the way, June has requested any additional information we may have on our boy. In the next couple of weeks, why don't you visit her and get some feedback on the new information in your report? Also, they started to grow the gumma in the lab. They have one in solution and it's about the size of a golf ball. You won't believe what happens to it around the time of the full moon. You might want to take a trip by the lab to take a look."

John stood up and said, "If you don't have anything else for me, that'll be all for now. I know you have a lot of things to take care of."

I shook my head yes and got up, grabbed my packet, and left.

Well, I was just leaving John's office and my head was on overload. I had to deal with these divorce papers and my wife. I have to talk to June about the new findings. And, most interestingly, I had to see what the new developments in the laboratory were with them growing the gumma samples. I can't say that this thing with my wife

was a total surprise, but it still hit and hurt hard. I rushed back to my apartment in town and prepared myself for a phone call. I thought the least I should do was to say goodbye and maybe give her the same opportunity.

As soon as I got to the apartment, I reviewed all the information in the packet. It was a standard no-contest divorce. She wanted the house and half of everything else. She also wanted me to pay half of child support until our daughters were out of college. It seemed entirely too fair and quick for this kind of document. I had this feeling that there was something else going on. I reached over for the phone and dialed her home number. I was a little surprised when a man answered the phone. I said, "This is Dr. Jordan Blane and I'd like to speak to Nonie, please."

The male voice yelled to someone in the room, "It's your husband!"

My wife came on the phone and said, "What do you want, Jordan?"

I said, "I received the packet from the attorney today and I am going to sign it and send it back."

She said, "Thank you."

Then I said, "Who's the guy who answered the phone?"

She said, "His name is Victor."

I asked, "Is he a permanent fixture in the home now?"

She said, "Well, yes, he has kind of become permanent. It's a long story, and it didn't start out that way."

Then I said, "I kind of would like to know what happened after all. Is that all my fault?"

She said, "It's no one's fault, Jordan. It's just what happened."

She took a pause and then related what it happened in the past year. "Since you've been on this quest, we have had two guards 24/7. One would go to work with me, and one would go to school with the girls. They said you were on a top priority mission which put us in danger. It was very hard continuing on with you not here. There was no one to pick up the slack and fill in for you with all the things you used to help us with. Victor was one of the guards. He would sit in the car all night long, watching the house. Occasionally, I would bring them out coffee in the morning when I left for work. Then we started having coffee in the kitchen before work. We started talking, got to know each other, and he started helping with things around the house. You left a big space in here when you left. We lost a father, a husband, and a helper. It had to get filled up sometime. Now we're a family again."

I was a little shocked at the finality of it, but I understood and knew that it was true. I knew there was nothing I could do and the only thing that I could think to say was, "I know this has been very difficult for you with my leaving and everything. I got involved in something very dangerous, and it was safer for you to be away from me. This wasn't the way I had planned for everything to turn out, but I do wish you wellness and happiness from now on."

She said, "Thank you. Goodbye."

I just sat there, putting the phone down. I was stunned. It was the end of twenty-plus years of love, of plans, of heartbreaks, and of everything that we had been with each other. Wow! I was so numb. I didn't know what to do. Actually, there was nothing to be done. It had already been done. And what I was feeling were the aftershocks.

It's amazing how your mind races in periods like this, trying to find an answer, the reason, a cause, someone or something to blame. You want to know why, as if that will change anything, except maybe settle your mind and give you something to focus on, something to hate, something to fight. I knew what I wanted to fight; it was that bastard wolf who drew me away from my family and made this happen. What I knew I needed to do was to get back on the trail, see June, see what she had to offer, visit the lab, and see if they have any ideas of how to fight this thing. I knew I had to figure out his next step. I had to get ahead of him. I had to post myself way in front of him, so he was coming to me.

I thought it best that I should go to the laboratory. This would give me a chance to share with June any additional information on the lab samples. I made an appointment for the next day, and they seemed anxious to show me what developed.

Ed Johnson greeted me when I arrived at the lab. He was excited and couldn't wait to tell me the findings and show me the films he had taken. He said the gumma were very viable and more easily grown in solution. He had grown four experimental cultures, and they all grew in the solution with amazing speed. He said most of the time they were floating about midway in the container, basically in the center of the solution. He thought this aided these tissues in getting nutrition from all sides. He said that these findings weren't all that unexplainable. However, three days before and after the full moon, there were changes that he could not explain and that seemed unnatural when one considers regular biological processes of life.

He said that at that time the tissues of the gumma, which had formed into a round ball, would start to swell two maybe three times their size. The tissues would also become heavier, much heavier than their increase in size could predict. They would cease to float and rest on the bottom of the container. Most astonishing was the fact that the whole glass container, tissue, and solution had an increase in weight. It was estimated that since the glass container and solution had not increased in weight or volume, the growing gumma had increased five or six times in weight. This process started three days before the full moon, peaked on the night of the full moon, and then return to somewhat normal three days later.

At that time, the regular growth cycle continued, and he had to change containers because of the gumma's increase in size. Still more amazing was that there was a differentiation in the tissues of the gummas. Hair, teeth, limb buds, and brain tissue were being formed.

The containers were in a row; each one had its own supply of nutrients and oxygen. They were about a foot apart. The one all the way to the right developed hair and brain tissue. The next in line developed teeth and hair. The next developed limb buds, hair, and lung tissue. And the final container appeared to develop organs and limb buds. It seemed, although they were not connected in any way, that the gumma are still attempting to develop a whole viable individual. In some way, it appears they are communicating with each other. Ed was extremely excited about this and wanted to show me the time-lapse videos of the process. It took me about twenty minutes to view his videos. I was frightened and very wary of what I have seen. Frightened because Ed couldn't wait for the next full moon to see how much more development would occur in his cultures. Wary because I just realized how much more potential for contamination and spread these creatures had, plus the fact that these gumma were probably pure werewolf. Could you imagine bringing these tissues into a complete individual? There would be no human tissue or qualities involved. Just pure werewolf tissue. I knew I had to talk to John about how far we should let these experiments proceed.

I called John right away as soon as I left the laboratory. I told him what I had seen and gave him my recommendations. I told him I thought the laboratory personnel was going to continue to grow their specimens until it became a complete individual. I told him I thought that the laboratory was in no way a secure enough place to continue such an experiment. I told him I didn't think it was wise to complete the growth as it seemed to be taking place. We didn't need more wolves running around, plus this wolf had the possibility of being a superwolf, since it was being grown from pure gumma. John thanked me for my observations and input and said that his direction in this experiment was to develop an immunosuppressive vaccine against these tissues. He was not going to allow these test tube jockeys to develop more problems for us. He said the immunologists were already there and were about to take over. I have to tell you, I felt much more relieved after this conversation.

I had to start to make preparations for my visit with June. It was impossible to walk into that place unannounced and be received. I had to make an appointment, and they would clear it with my supervisor, and finally with their lieutenant commander. This might take four or five days, so I had to start the process as soon as possible. Then when it was all finished, I could get a flight out. I was kind of glad I didn't have a secretary to do the scheduling for me. This busy work helped keep my mind off other things. I knew I was only starting to feel the effects of the divorce. But, for some reason, I was the kind of guy who didn't like to face up to all of this emotional turmoil all at once. The memories, the pain, the what-ifs, they can all come later. Right now, I'm a hunter on the trail of a dangerous and cunning prey. I just kept telling myself that. Then I focused on the other things that didn't bother me so much. I was so amazed I could work on the hunting and killing of that creature, but not on the loss of my wife and family. For me, maybe it is easier to face hunting, killing, and death than that part of my life that involves the loss of relationships and love.

The scheduling finally came through, and six days later I'm going through security to see June. All the construction that was going on before seemed to have been completed and cleaned up. When I got to where June was being kept, there were more personnel and offices and electronic controls that I had remembered before. June's apartment had been reinforced and expanded.

There was now an exercise area, entertainment center, and several other rooms were added. Some of those new rooms had heavy locking doors. I supposed they were there to keep June more contained during her full moon time.

The whole area looked more open. There was a reception desk close to where you entered June's apartment. There was an area of about thirty feet were there was a minimum amount of glass and bars. It made one room be just as much a part of the other. It would be very easy for people to have a regular conversation, and yet be on different sides of the bars and glass. This appeared very different from the reinforcement that I saw last time until I looked up at the ceiling and saw large plates of glass and ironed rods that could be dropped down at any time.

The soldier sitting at the reception desk waved me over and called me by name. He told me that I could meet with June in her apartment living room. I would have to give up my firearm for safety reasons before I entered the area, though. Then he spoke to the microphone, saying, "Miss June, Dr. Blaine is here to see you."

Then he turned to me and said, "Go over to the door. I'll buzz you in."

By that time, June was already over to the door with their hand-out, saying, "Welcome, Dr. Blaine. So nice to see you again. Please have a seat on the couch in the living room."

I took a seat on the couch, and she sat across from me in an upholstered chair. I remarked to her as I was sitting down that the place looked much more airy.

She said, "Yes, they were making renovations, so I made some recommendations which would make living more tolerable and more secure. I don't know if you noticed the additional bars that can come down from the ceiling. They can be activated from the outside or by me from the inside."

I smiled and thought to myself, *Very clever. She feels she must be more knowledgeable and prepared than her guardians.*

I immediately started to think about how much I should relate to June about my experiences in New Orleans. It seemed like it was up to me, since John hadn't told me to withhold anything from June that was in my report. I knew I didn't want to tell her about the gumma in the laboratory experiments. I thought that might be too frightening for her to know the fact that we were experimenting with tissues from creatures like her.

She got right down to the inquisition about what new information had come across. She had heard that I was out of town and had suspected I was following up some leads. I told her that I was and that I had uncovered evidence of another wolfman. Immediately, she seemed startled, excited, and curious all at once. "Please tell me everything," she said.

So I related everything to her step by step, from my following up the newspaper article, the initial coverup from the Cajun community, to their final confession about what was really going on. Then I told her about the call from the Southern wolfman. I told her that he had finally called me and told me that there was much more going on with my case than I have ever suspected. I related to her his estimation of the Northern wolf. I told her about how the only way for a werewolf's line to become stronger is for two wolves to mate and have a child. I told her about the difficulty of raising such a child and that had not been done in many, many years.

June just looked at me, stunned and amazed. This was the first time I had ever seen her taken aback without any reply or admission. She just sat in front of me expressionless, in deep thought, shaking her head up and down as if she understood. Her demeanor had completely changed. She wasn't that smiling confident young woman who appeared to have all the answers who was sitting in front of me minutes before. She looked at me and said, "Well, this explains an awful lot, especially why I'm still alive. But it doesn't explain why you're still here. I still need more information to see what part you have to play in all this."

Right then, I saw that her thinking was so far ahead of mine. I had somehow come to conclusion that I was either smarter or luckier than those who had come in contact with our wolfman. I thought because I was part of this investigation unit that I had an extra layer of protection covering me. It hadn't occurred to me that I was another pawn in his gain for power and control. I was probably kept alive for his evil purposes. That, at least, is what June was proposing.

Right then, June did something amazing that I had not expected. She reached over and grabbed my hand and squeezed gently, saying, "I think we are involved more than either of us know or suspect. I really feel an attachment to you, like I have felt for no other person. You are the only one that I can be completely truthful with and probably you understand me more than anyone else."

I was so startled. Not only did I feel so physically and emotionally attracted to her, but it felt like some power had come into me. I didn't feel like I was my own man anymore. There was someone else in me, influencing me, directing my attention and desires. I managed to smile a little and shook my head as if I agreed, but I felt like I'd been hit by something powerful and sure and direct.

Wow! I thought. *She is mesmerizing me. She is planning on using me somehow.* My mind was racing, reaching out for reasons and explanations of what was going on. I thought maybe she really likes me and wants me to be her boyfriend. Then I thought, *Not a chance. There are too many other handsome strong young men around here.* Then I thought maybe she's mesmerizing them, also. Then I realized that probably she could get out of here anytime she wanted with her ability to influence, excite, and make us move to her will. Then I wondered if she could read minds. Probably not.

I decided to quickly change the subject. I asked, "Do you think he is keeping me alive for some reason?"

She said, looking me directly in the face, "I am very sure he is. Otherwise, you would have been gone a long time ago."

I asked June, "How do I capture or kill him or confront him? How do I find him?"

She said, "There is only one way. You have to put yourself in his head and figure out what all of his next moves might be. Then you choose one and place yourself way ahead of him, hoping that you chose the right option. If you did choose rightly, he will catch up to you. The chances that you can figure him out are slim., but the fact that you are out there waiting and looking and getting reports will provide some degree of possibility that you will run into each other. If you follow his trail, you will never get ahead of him. If you follow the trail, he will lead you were he wants you to go. He will be orchestrating you rather than you trapping him. This is the best advice and the only advice I can give you at this time. It's like I said, I need a lot more information."

Then almost immediately, she switched the focus of the conversation and said, "I noticed you don't wear your wedding band anymore."

I said, "Yes, I'm afraid my wife has decided to divorce me."

Then she said, "I'm sorry you're having to go through that at this time. It's got to be hard to go through such a thing."

I just shook my head yes and didn't say anything.

Then she said, "They have allowed me to have a couple of friends. They come in a couple of times a week. We talk and play games. I occasionally let them win. I am learning to relate to young adults. The male, so far, he is so predictable. Although sometimes I just do not know what is going to come out of his mouth before he speaks, every now and then he does surprise me. I am not sure if it's because he is so irrational at times that there is no normal thought process or his hormones, which are not tied to the thought process, are interacting with his mind. He does, however, seem to be genuine and truthful. Whatever comes out of him appears to be the way he really feels or thinks. He is always smiling when he comes to visit, and I think he really enjoys being here. It is very easy to relate to him on some levels, but he hasn't a hint about what he's supposed to be doing other than having fun and stroking his own ego.

"The other two are girls in their early twenties. They are manipulative and deviceive. Everything they say or do strives to maintain the image they have manufactured for themselves. And everything else in the world is viewed as supporting or taking away from that image. In order to really communicate with them, you have to communicate with their image construct. I do see a lot of potential in them to mature beyond where they are now. There may be a time when they really know who they are and aren't afraid to act like it. Whenever they come in at some point, they always steer the conversation into what the latest rock stars or movie stars are doing. I don't care about any of that kind of stuff, so the conversations are usually between the two girls in front of me. They do this all the time, as if the knowledge of the antics of these merchandised people gives them some kind of personal power or status. They are such prodigals, wasting their time and energy on things that to me seem to give no lasting reward since every couple of days all the stories change.

"I don't mean to seem to be too critical of these young ladies. They are fun to be around, and I have learned a lot from them, especially about your species. They are much more mature and self-directed than their male counterpart. I'm sure this helps them a lot when it comes to selecting a mate. Also, they don't mind watching movies and soap operas about love and romance. Robert, the young male, cannot contend with the same level of emotional and situational conflict that the girls can, and he has to run away every time. From what I see on the television and computer, many men are like that. What do you think?"

I said, "I guess so." But I knew instantly that she was talking about what she was seeing in me. I was feeling like I wanted to run away and not discuss the subject anymore. She was just looking at me and smiling like she wanted more of a retort from me. I was kind of smiling sheepishly, although I sensed a part of me wanting to cry out and say, "I'm hurting so bad about my family and the divorce I can't even think about it." The only thing that came out was, "Going through what I'm going through right now is really hard to speak about."

She stopped smiling and shook her head and said, "Well, if you ever want to share some with me, I'll be glad to listen and help you any way I can."

I said, "Thank you."

In her perfect timing, she changed the subject again. "Anyway, it is pleasant just to have company, you included."

I said, "Thank you very much. I enjoyed being here with you, also."

She related that she would like to make our visits more regular since they seem to be informative for both of us. I said I agree and that I would try to get over to see her more often. "I don't think John will mind," she said.

Then changing the subject again, she said that a couple of weeks ago she detected a sent in the air. She said she knew instinctively it was male wolfman and that she had never smelt anything like that before. She knew it was the one who made her. I told her that the Southern wolfman had told me that his kind could smell another up to fifty miles away. I told her the next time that she experiences that scent she should call me or John right away. All of a sudden, I had a thought in my mind that our wolfman may have been scouting and exploring the areas around the fort. He may be planning something in the future. June was in danger. What kind of danger, I was not sure, but I knew we had to protect her.

I knew I had to get to John right away with this information, so I got up, said goodbye, excused myself, and started to walk toward the door.

June said, "I know you've got to be going, but please come again soon." She reached out and shook my hand firmly and waved goodbye.

Immediately after leaving June, I contacted John from my car in the parking lot. I related to him what June had told me about detecting the scent of the wolfman. I also told him that she thought that this was the one who had infected her. I also recapped to John the fact that a werewolf could smell another from fifty miles away. John said that he thought this was very significant information and he would be giving me his take on it, but he wanted a few days to put his head around it and determine its full significance. He told me to come back to Washington and to be taking some time off. He would be getting in touch with me as soon as he figured out all of the implications of what I had told him.

It was the fourth day since John and I had talked. I didn't enjoy the time off like I thought I would. I had too many emotions and memories running around inside me. I tried to stay busy doing unnecessary things, like arranging my files, cleaning out my closet, and getting the oil changed in the car. None of it really kept me from thinking about my family, wife, and kids. I was very glad when John finally called me and told me to come in to see him at once.

It was only a twenty-minute drive to our main office. It was an 8:00 a.m. meeting so it was good there would be a lot of work for the rest of the day. A lot of the important mentors, advisers, and administrators were already there hanging around John's office. A couple were just exiting as I got to his doorway. Somehow, I got the sense that they had all already talked to John and that I was probably the last one to get this important information.

As I got to the entrance to his office, John waved me in and told me to sit down. John said, "We have been putting together all the information that you have told us. We didn't realize it, but June can give us a significant advantage in finding this fiend. Her abilities are superior to anything we have. We had no idea that her sense of smell was so keen. We want to use her as a hound dog—no pun intended—to track him down. If she can smell fifty miles in any direction, that's a circle one hundred miles wide that we can cover. If we can put her in a mobile unit, we can cover about 500 miles a day. That's a lot of territory. And once we get his scent, we can track him down. Everyone I've talked to thinks it's a good idea and wants to go with it. I hope you're on board with it, also."

I came in a little depressed and not too invigorated, but now I was excited and energized. I told John I thought it was a great idea. This is really the first time we can really go after him. All the other times we were just following his trail, being led around, following a ghost that was long gone. I asked, "What did June think about the idea?"

John said, "I haven't discussed it with her yet. I hope you'll be able to help me in getting her to go along with our plan. We're developing a very secure trailer in which she can be transported. It will have all the luxuries of her home and then some. She will have a chance to get out in the fresh air and see a lot of the countryside. She will be protected by armed guards inside and the whole convoy of trailers and vehicles with armed guards with the latest detection equipment. The President doesn't even travel with this much security. I will be there, as well as you. I will personally guarantee her safety. And if anything happens that compromises her safety, we will bring in the armed helicopters and fly her right back. I'm asking you to discuss it with her because I think you have a good rapport with her."

What it sounded like, he was suggesting a field trip with June. I thought it might be fun, and our searching for the wolf's scent might put us hot on his trail. I told John I would go see June as soon as possible and discuss the whole program with her. He said to get right on it and that they were going ahead with the design of her trailer. I shook my head yes, understanding that we were already going for and already on board with this plan. I stepped into the outer offices and made an appointment to see June as soon as possible. Within five minutes, I heard John's secretary get a call from the fort asking for his approval to set me an appointment. I was going in the next day.

I arrived early, went through the necessary processing stations, and saw June was already waiting for me in her reception area, sitting on one of the smaller couches. I walked in and said, "I bet you didn't think you'd see me so soon."

She said, "Please, have a seat. It was a nice surprise to hear last evening that you were coming to visit this morning. I bet you have something interesting to tell me."

I said, "Yes, I do, and I think you'll really like what I'm going to tell you."

She said, "Please explain."

I told her that John and his people thought it was extremely significant that she could detect the wolfman scent, especially from such a far distance, and that they had devised a plan where we could put her in a mobile laboratory and search for him using her ability to detect his scent. I also told her about the mobile laboratory which looked like a trailer. It would be very secure and safe and have an entourage of armed guards and investigators. She would have every convenience that she can imagine, and she would not have to do anything other than to get out in the fresh air and let us know if she can smell his scent.

After I said that, she sat back on the couch with a partial smile on her face. Smiling, she looked at me and said, "I told you something that made me feel very uneasy and perhaps put me in danger, and you have turned it around to use against him. You have found one of his few weaknesses. Congratulations, you are really going on the offensive. I thought you would never see my potential. That in me he had created a way to get to him. I would be happy to join you on your road trip to seek out and destroy this killer. But there was one thing you must know. If I can smell him, he can smell me. So we must develop some sort of procedure for hiding and masking my own scent."

I said, "I'm sure that is very doable, since even modern-day hunters have commercial products which they use to mask their sent while on a hunt." I also said that we would get working on that right away and was sure that we could come up with something even more efficient than what was available to the average person.

She said, "When do you think this can take place?" I told her we were already starting to make plans for the construction of her trailer, and this would be the most time-consuming part of the project. We already have the rest of the equipment and manpower for the convoy. "I think we're looking to at least a month away."

She looked at me and said, "Dr. Blaine, please tell John and everybody involved thank you for having this much faith in me. I see this project helping everyone involved in this case. And if we can just discover the direction he is moving, we have a chance of getting ahead of him and perhaps setting a trap. I am very excited about this."

I related that I was also excited, and that I would tell John and the rest of the crew that she was on board with the plan. I smiled and got up to leave, and she stood and reached out her hand to shake goodbye. I grabbed her hand to shake, and she gently squeezed my hand with both of her hands and said, "I'm glad they sent you to tell me this great news. I think we have a good rapport and understanding of what must be done to catch this rogue wolf."

Right then, I felt a surge of excitement and passion go through my body right into my stomach. I thought, *She is probably mesmerizing me again, but what a thrill.* I walked out of her abode with a little smile on my face.

I called John from the car and told him that she was all on board and that she looks forward to getting started. He said, "Good idea. I knew you could get this going." And I told him about her concerns about her own scent. He said he would get the best minds in the country working on it and that he didn't think it would be a problem. Then he said he wanted me to come in a couple of days and review the plans for the trailer, specifically see if I could make any suggestions. He also said that he wasn't sure, but he might run them by June, also, since she was so instrumental in the reconstruction of her living quarters. He said, "Stay in the area. I will be in touch."

Well, I knew a couple more days off would probably be good for me—going to the gym, washing the car, watching television, movies on TV. Yeah, really good.

It wasn't a couple of days, actually. It was five days until John got in touch with me. He said that he had emailed me the plans and had wanted to know if I had any ideas or improvements that could be added to support the purpose and functionality of the trailer. I told him I would get on it right away.

When I pulled it up on the screen, my first impression was that it was a ten-wheeled portable tank. It was bulletproof all the way around, with large sections of bulletproof glass supported with steel rods. There were three compartments. The middle was the largest and equipped with every luxury and electronic device for one's entertainment. It had a sleeping area and living area with television and stereo. There was a small kitchen with a refrigerator. There was also a small room with only a cot and water basin. The room was all steel with recess cameras, lighting, and a small see-through box on the door. Nothing was going to get in or out of that room once the door was locked since it was enclosed in a half inch chrome steel.

The other two compartments were small, with just enough space for three to four men. These compartments were located at each end of the trailer. Like the middle compartment, both of these compartments had an entrance from the outside. They both also had an entrance in June's living quarters. There was a lot of surveillance equipment which focused on the inside and outside of the trailer.

There was air conditioning and air regulation equipment. There was equipment which would bring in untreated air from the outside, specifically for June. They were also air exchange ducts to remove the air inside June's compartment which would be treated with filtration, with liquids and electronic devices to render it pure and inert.

There was also provided something that I thought June would enjoy. They were able to open up picture windows on either side of the trailer so you could view the countryside. And I think most important was the fact that the sunroof could be retracted to let light in so June could get a suntan through the large metal bars. About the only thing I thought that was missing were four men riding on top with machine guns, but I think the rest of the convoy will supply that need. That information is probably on a need to know basis, and I don't need to know it just now. Although I know, somehow, I will be involved.

I called John and told him that everything looked very good for what we wanted to do. I did mention that I thought the trailer needed more outside security other than a few cameras pointing out the sides. John said there would be two troop carriers leading and following the trailer. They would have full view of the trailer at all times. Also in the convoy would be several vehicles which carried specialized detection equipment. They would be able to detect a heat signature of anything larger than normal moving faster than normal up to 300 yards away. There were going to be six vehicles in the convoy, in addition to the trailer and its carrier. Then he said, "I'd like you to print out the plans and run them by June to see if she has any suggestions." I said okay and got on it right away.

Once again, I had to go through the procedure to see June. Luckily, I got in the next day. June was her normally perky attentive self who welcomed the plans with much enthusiasm. As she reached out for the plans, she said, "I hope you're going to be part of the road trip."

I said, "I believe I am."

She said, "It will be extremely important that we move very quickly once we detect him. If he understands what we are doing, he will move so fast that we will never get a hold of him." Then she looked at the plans and said, "These look very intricate. It will take some time to go over them. Can you come back tomorrow and I'll let you know what I think?"

I said sure. As I got up to leave, she once again grabbed my hand and shook it, and I left.

The next day, when I returned, I was very surprised that she had a list of recommendations. They were twenty or so on the list, with the most important being listed first. They were things, like a need for bulletproof tires, a panic button so she could immediately notify those in control to shut everything down, a female guard being on hand for more personal feminine requirements, and a chance to have personal visitors, be they guards or investigators, so she would have someone to talk to and perhaps play games with on the trip. The other requests were less primary, like being supplied with a pair of binoculars, window and bed sizes, the décor, and could she be able to shut off one of the restroom cameras when she was on the commode? The one on the floor looking up rather than the ceiling camera. I took the request and got up to leave, and she said, "Dr. Blaine, I don't have any more visitors scheduled for today. Is there any possibility you could stay for a couple of hands of cards or some of the other games?" She was smiling, and I really wanted to stay, but I told her that I wanted to get the request back to John as soon as possible. But next visit I would definitely schedule in more time for a little fun. She said "Thank you, Dr. Blaine" and waved goodbye, as I walked out of her apartment.

Rather than just take a picture of June's request and emailing them to John, I wanted to talk to him on the phone and see how far the project had gone. On the phone, John told me to do exactly what I was going to do and that was email him the request as soon as possible. He said that the trailer frame and inside structure had been completed. What they were going to start working on now were the inside and outside walls, electronics, and all associated equipment. I asked him when it should be finished, and he said, if there are no more problems, in about three weeks. He said the crews were working twenty-four hours a day and that, of course, this was top secret from now on. We were only to use a secure Internet connection for the delivery of any of the information because of the possibility of being hacked. He said he had already notified June of the same.

Three weeks wasn't long at all, especially for this type of project. It would probably give me some time to visit June and play some games. I would have to notify John, but I don't think he would mind since he wanted me to build a rapport with her, anyway. I thought I would schedule the next visit in a couple of days. In the meantime, it was probably a good idea to go to the store and shop for some card games she was not familiar with. That way, I might have a chance of being a little competition for her.

I was about to make it an appointment to see June when John gave me an urgent call to see him. It seems some important developments had happened in the laboratory and he wanted to discuss them with me. I thought it had to do with the immunologists developing a serum against the gumma. I couldn't have been more offtrack.

As soon as I got John's office, his secretary buzzed me into his office. John was visibly upset as he related happenings in the laboratory. It seems he sent some investigators into the lab to see how the immunologists were progressing. What they found out was that all of the laboratory personnel were intently working on continuing to grow the gumma. He said that the gumma have continually grown and developed into four parts of an individual. The four containers of the tissue had developed into very recognizable head, thorax, abdomen, and legs. Not only that, but the containers were covered with growths of tendrils which reached out to communicate with the other containers. They were soon going to connect up to become a complete individual.

It appeared that all the laboratory workers are under some kind of spell or were mesmerized and persuaded that the growth of a complete individual was their main project. Even the immunologists who were there to develop antibodies against the gumma were mentally taken over to believe they had to complete the individual. John felt that it was some form of mental telepathy which cause them to exhibit a new reality and a new purpose for the project. As a result of these findings, the project was completely shut down. The four containers were stored in a secure building at -73 degrees Fahrenheit. They are under twenty-four-hour video surveillance to make sure there is no growth, now or in the future.

The personnel in the lab, who became increasingly aggressive and violent when they found the project was being shut down, have all been sequestered at a secure facility. There they are being observed and tested to see how permanent and how long they remain turned over to this new reality that they were so intently embracing. John said that not only were they intent on completing to grow the individual, but they were exhibiting emotional attachment to the growths in the containers They had actually fallen in love with it. They were sad and sobbing when they were taken away from their experiment. John thought the implications were astounding and very dangerous.

He asked me if I had seen any evidence of June using this type of power. I told him I wasn't sure because it could probably only be detected in the most extreme circumstance of human relations. In my own relationship with June, everything seemed to be cordial and above board. The relationship with her friends and guards were normal and friendly. If there was any mental coercion going on, it would be very hard to detect. The only real changes that had occurred with June were the renovations to her apartment which included increasing the area and making the area more secure. This, I thought, was mutually advantageous to both ours and her situations. John agreed and told me to remember that she also submitted a lot of the renovations which were approved across the board. And even now, she is helping us to develop a trailer to go out and hunt her opponent, Much of which has been approved.

He said, "In light of this laboratory takeover, the implications of her having this type of control over us is mind blowing. How would one know if they were being controlled? How would you even detect that there was a controlling influence about?" John said something very startling, "I think from now on we will have to assume that there is a controlling power that June, her opponent, and any other like individual have a controlling power that can be used against us. As best we can, we must test every interaction with these individuals as to where it's going, what it means, and whose best interest is it in. I think we're going to have to increase our department with a whole new intelligence division. The fact that June is alive and well and maturing. The fact that you saw him and survived and are now working for us. And the fact that we are going out seeming to be more prepared than ever before and searching for him all may not be our plan. We might be working for someone else's agenda. We now have an awful lot to consider."

Then John said, "In the interactions that you have with June, be aware she may be influencing you and those around her. Keep your eyes and ears open and report to me immediately any suggestion of mental coercion that may be going on around her and by her."

I told John I certainly would consider and work on these new revelations. As I walked out, I was very devastated. I was starting to think that June liked me and that we were enjoying each other's company. And now there was the possibility that this was some mental implantation from her in my mind and not my own intuitive instincts. I was feeling like I had lost control of my job and all the pertinent relationships in my life. I had almost got to my car when John's secretary was yelling at me from the other side of the parking lot to come back in. I turned around quickly and jogged back to the building.

She quickly led me back to John's office where he waved me in and pointed for me to sit down in the chair I had previously occupied. He asked me if I remembered Temo's wife, the woman who had lost her husband and son. I nodded yes, and he continued, saying that they had offered her witness protection. She had refused choosing to go back to Italy and living with her relatives in a place called Terni. It was a northern Italian town in the Alps. It was thought that she might be safe there out of the country. After all, she had never seen anything. Anyway, the report had just come in that she and her family were slaughtered by some unknown beast. John was pretty sure it was our wolfman and had dispatched a couple of agents to go there and investigate and bring back proof to back up our assumptions.

John looked me straight in the face and said, "I wanted you to know this so it would continually reinforce in your mind that we are in a war where our opponents are smarter, stronger, and more powerful than we are. We, however, have the numbers of people working against them and more eyes to report to a central agency and constant twenty-four-hour investigation force. There is a trail out there, and we will pick it up. It's impossible to live in this world without making some imprint, some brushing against society. Someone has had to have interacted with this person. You have a relationship with June. She is the only connection we have at this point. I would like you to continue to interact with her, be friends but always keep in mind she may be trying to manipulate us."

I shook my head and said, "Yes, I will continue to work with June." Then I looked at John and said, "This wolfman never stops, does he?"

John looked up and said, "This is the way it's been for the past four or five years. No survivors, no witnesses. No one who even knows about him survives. June, you, and your family are the only exceptions. You are still alive, and we don't know why. And it is true that by you being here we have learned more about our killer than we have ever known before. So be very careful and keep up the good work."

I told John I certainly would try my best, and I left his office.

On the way back to my car, I felt there was a lot of pressure on me. John had just told me that I was the central key that had unlocked this investigation. Yet I was confronting creatures who are so far superior to me that I felt they might be orchestrating me, rather than me investigating them. And there was no help from anyone. I had to do it all myself. I had to just do it; let it play itself out, not knowing how much I was being used and given information to direct me and my group to what they wanted to accomplish.

It also occurred to me that June's presentation and suggestion that the wolfman was an adversary was totally false. They could be working together, coming from different sides to accomplish the same end. Wow!

Just the thought of that idea made me feel very uneasy. How would anyone ever know, until all the parts came together at the end, the time when they have accomplished all that they started to do?

I knew I had to make another appointment to see June. I would play some card games with her and get to know her better, if possible. I would have to not let her know that anything had changed in the way I looked at her and the way I related to her. This might not be an easy task since she seemed to be very perceptive.

I had parked my car and was walking to see June. I had been put off a few days to see her since it was the time of the full moon. During that time—three days before and three days after—she was totally isolated and not permitted visitors. I have three card games that I had picked up. I was pretty sure she had never played any of these and, actually, neither had I. One of them was called Rook and it looked pretty interesting.

Upon entering the area of her apartment, I noticed how attractive she was and that she was out of her designated area, leaning on the guard's desk and talking to him. They were both smiling and laughing like you would expect young adults to be doing in a pub. I was sure this was a breach of protocol, but this was not the place to say anything. Besides, I was feeling a little jealous that she was having such a good time with that young man. As soon as she saw me, she came over, saying, "Dr. Blaine, I have been waiting for you. It's so nice to see you again." She then grabbed me by the arm, wrapping her arm around mine and leading me into her apartment. I couldn't help thinking right then that she had really expanded her control over the area, far beyond her living quarters. I wondered how far she could take it.

We sat down together on the couch and went through the games I had brought. She was interested in playing them, especially the one called Rook. She suggested that it would be much more fun and competitive if we had more players. She asked if I could come when her friends were there so we could play card games together. I said I thought it was a good idea. Well, knowing that she would probably beat me in every game and if there were more people there, we would have a longer time to play. She said, "Great, my friends will be here in two days for lunch. Could you come around 1:00 p.m."

I said, "It's a deal."

Having put away the subject of the games, she quickly asked me, "How is the trailer coming?"

I told her it was about two weeks till completion. She asked if I had seen it yet and had they approved of her improvements. I told her I had not seen it, but it was my understanding that most of her improvements were included.

She smiled and said, "That sounds wonderful. I can't wait to get going on this. Now instead of him coming for me, we will be coming for him."

I shook my head yes and said I hope that's the way it turns out.

June looked at me and said, "This is the only way it can go and must go." She looked at me straight in the face and said, "I have been thinking a lot about what you have said and what has happened. I think the only reason I'm around is that he wants to breed with me. If we don't stop him soon, he will find his way in here or unleash a torrent of soldiers like himself to take over this place. If either of these happens, I don't think I will be around very long."

As I looked at her, I grabbed her hand and told her that she shouldn't worry because we are going to protect her. After all, look at all the renovations that we have made, just to better effect that purpose.

She said, "I know you're trying but you have no idea of the amount of the evil and destructive force he is capable of." Then she squeezed my hand tightly, looked in my eyes, and that was it. I was in love. Or at least, felt the feeling of being in love. It was amazing. I never thought I would feel that way again and with the intensity stronger than I could ever remember.

All the while, there was this little voice in me saying this probably isn't real. But I didn't care. This was a once-in-a-lifetime experience, and I was going to go with it for now. Her hand still in mine, I pulled her close, so close her lips almost touched mine.

She said, "Yes, but not here. The guards will report us."

I backed off and asked, "What's happening?"

She said, "You know when a man and woman like each other and want to have a relationship with each other? It's a natural flow of things. But with our circumstances, it shouldn't happen right now."

I looked at her, and she had a forced smile, with tears rolling down her cheeks. At that moment, part of me wanted to take her by the hand and fight my way out of that place and take her with me. The other part of me wanted to get up and run and never look back because I was so much under her control. But I surprised myself; I just patted her hand and told her that a lot of things still have to happen and that we will just have to wait and see how things go. She didn't say anything; she just shook her head yes.

I felt like I should go, so I stood up and said, "I think we've covered a lot for today. I think I'll be going. We have a game date in two days. I'll see you then."

She shook her head yes and just sat there as I left. I say I left, but I know part of me was still there with her. She had really gotten to me. How could I even tell John about this? He may want to spoil this. He might want to shut this all down. He might want to stop the trailer expedition. There were too many questions and no good answers. Sometimes it's just better to do nothing, say nothing, and think nothing. And right now, that's the place where I am.

We had three different game dates with June and her friends. They were always there by the time I arrived. There were two girls, a guy, and June and me. We played all the games, but Rook turned out to be the most popular. I don't know how she managed it, but the guys always seem to win. This is my take on the situation. I'm not a good cardplayer and don't even like playing cards. The other young man was entirely too young to have any experience, and I understood that this is his very first time playing any of the games. Yet we were winning almost all the time. I think I'll have to thank June for this winning streak, although I have no idea how she orchestrated it.

As far as June's relationship with me, she played it very cool. She treated me just like each of her other friends. She introduced me and called me by my first name and immediately fit me in like I was one of the group. She never sat next to me at the table, usually directly across from me. Whenever I arrived, it was like a signal that we should all start to arrange the table to play cards. I think June arranged for her friends to arrive a couple of hours before I got there. That way, they could talk about all their young adult/teenage inter-ests. This was fine with me, since there was no way I could relate with these kids on those subjects. Playing cards, though, was something that we could all do and remain interested in together. So we played cards. But my main interest was not the card game as much as it was June. She was gorgeous, and I was going through something that I could only describe as teenage infatuation. Every time she looked at me or spoke my name, I got a funny feeling in the pit of my stomach. I was so amazed at how she could affect this in me, a professional man in his mid-fifties who had thought he had put these kinds of emotions to rest a long time ago. I thought it was best to just let it happen and let her think she is in control. This way, I might be able to see where she's going on this. Anyway, it wasn't so bad feeling so young and alive and inspired.

We had a couple of weeks before the trailer would be completed. This was a good way to spend the time while we were waiting for its completion. On this, I was waiting for John's call to let me know we were ready for the expedition.

Officially, this time with June was my work, and I was embracing it with much enthusiasm.

It was about three and a half weeks when John got back to me. He said that everything was ready to go and that I should report to the convoy in two days. He said that he got in touch with June and that she was ready. I was to bring everything I needed to be on expedition for about three weeks. I was to arrive at the convoy site a little before 7:00 a.m. Everything had been planned and was put on a computer. We all had flowcharts of where we were supposed be and what we were to be doing for fixed periods of time. He said I could download a paper copy on my personal computer. Having done that, I found out that I was assigned to eight different stations at different times in the convoy. My time was pretty well taken up, about ten to twelve hours a day.

I arrived about 6:45 a.m. and went directly to the mobile control center. John was there and beckoned for me to come in. My first station was to be manning the video camera security system. John sent me down in front of the screens and explained how it worked.

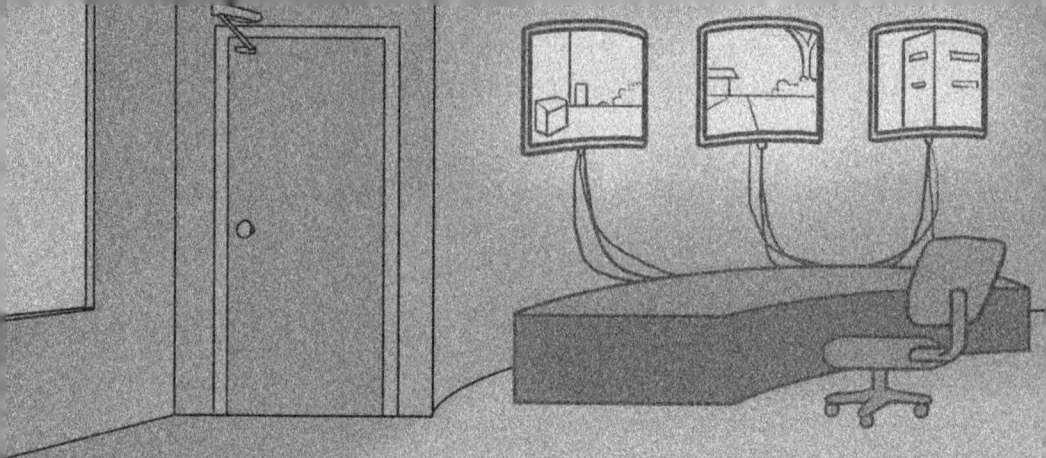

Even though the control center followed June's trailer, it received video coverage from inside the trailer, from inside the control booth in the trailer, front, back, and sides of the trailer, as well as coverage around the outside of the control center. This was just video coverage. There was also a radar and heat sensitive unit which picked up movement and life signs outside. John explained that I was going to be used in every station of the convoy. He wanted me to be one of his go-to men. In case of an emergency, I would be able to fill in anywhere. He also said that June had been in her trailer since yesterday. They wanted her to get comfortable and run a bunch of security checks with her there before they moved out. He also related that a couple of my stations would be in the trailer with June and her matron. This was done because he wanted me to keep up my relationship with June and to get direct feedback from her as to how she thought things were going. I said. "I understand."

John further pointed out that the convoy consisted of five vehicles. There were two Chevy Suburbans which would lead. There was a tractor-trailer which pulled June's specially-equipped trailer. The tractor-trailer had its own small control center in the cab just behind the driver. The trailer it pulled was June's living quarters which had an observation booth with three stations and it was the only way in or out of trailer. The main mobile control center, which we were in, was electronically outfitted with cameras, sensors, communication equipment, and eight personnel in a special RV. Finally, there was another Chevy Suburban which contained observational equipment and a lot of firepower. John didn't elaborate on the type of firepower, but I knew it was more than just handguns and rifles.

John further elaborated on the staffing. There was a total of sixty people involved in the expedition. There would be eight-hour shifts using twenty at a time, with a lot of flexibility to shifts if they will need to be increased in time. The other forty workers would be housed in three mobile trailers which would follow up ten to fifteen miles behind. These were rest trailers with both observational and defensive capabilities. Being so close, they were also to be used as a defensive backup in case of an attack. They were about ten minutes away. John said there was also an army helicopter team of about thirty men who were on 24/7 standby. I looked at John and said, "I think we'll be in really big trouble if we have to call them." Pointing to my pistol in my shoulder holster, I said, "I think we can take care of anything that comes along." John just smiled and shook his head yes.

I was so astonished that John was showing me all this. I told him I was amazed at how much he had accomplished in such a short time.

John said, "This isn't just our department. A lot of other people very high up have come on board with this project. They may not understand all the intricacies of who and what we are fighting, but they do know that it is contagious and a national threat. The CDC and Army are both on board. In fact, the Army is the one carrying out the supply detail for the convoy. Every 200 to 400 miles, they will supply us with gas, food, water, and anything else that we deem necessary. So if there's anything that you forgot or may need extra, don't hesitate to tell my administrative assistant and it will be included in the next delivery."

I said okay and started checking out all the screens with the cameras for monitoring the convoy. What was going on was people going and coming from their different stations. I could even see June sitting in her trailer, talking to her matron. I was very excited to get this expedition on the road. We had the equipment, the manpower, and we had June to lead us. All we had to do was to get within fifty miles of our wolfman.

Just then, four or five soldiers came in to see John. They saluted John when they saw him, and he saluted back. I didn't think we were part of the army, but maybe we were even something higher up. They all went over in a corner, and John ordered coffee for them. They all huddled together around a table and talked quietly. No one could hear what they were saying but it appeared they were planning to get ready to go, as well as supplying our convoy. As they were leaving, I noticed there were at least two generals, a coronel, and a couple of other assistants.

My next station was with June and her matron in the trailer. When I came in, June was all bubbly and happy to see me. She ran over and grabbed me by the hand and set me down on the couch next to her. The matron asked if I would like any coffee or anything to drink. I said no. June said she was very happy to see me and was glad that I was included in the convoy and able to spend some time with her. She was very excited to get started, and everything was going as planned. She said that she was so happy to finally be out in the fresh air. There were so many smells and sensations that she was receiving. For example, she said she sensed me when I first drove up to the convoy three hours ago. She said it's not just me but everyone in the convoy has a different smell and identity and she's having trouble cataloguing all of us before we get moving. I thought to myself she already knows more about what's going on around here than anyone. I really hope she can't read minds.

June and I were sitting alone on the couch. I noticed the matron without being told took a seat in the far side of the trailer. June leaned over to me and said, "There's something I really want to talk to you about. When we finally get a scent of the one we're hunting, there is only one way we can really get him. If we just follow the scent, we will always be following. He knows that and he will probably start to sense we're getting close. The only way to get him is for you to leave the convoy once we find what direction he is going. You'll have to go far ahead of where he's proceeding. Then you'll have to start coming back on him. Chances are good that you will run into him. You may have to do this several times, but you will eventually catch him. We know he stays on the roads and there're only so many roads up North. This is our advantage, and you have to take it. If he suspects what we are doing, he will attack us or make an army of his kind to attack us. Jordan, if that happens, I don't think I will be around for very long. If I have a future and if we have a future, you have to get to him and kill him."

She still had me by the hand, and I was looking into her eyes and I knew exactly what I had to do. I would tell John and I think he would agree with her plan, but if he didn't, I think I would still go anyway. For me, it was like I was born for this. This hunt was the culmination of my whole life. There was nothing else. Every sense, every part of my body and mentality was dedicated and focused to do this. I had to kill the wolfman.

It was time to go to the next station which was my resting time in the resting trailer following the caravan. I thought it was important to go talk to John about June's plan to kill the wolfman. During the hourly stop/slowdown when the workers would switch stations, I walked over to John's central control trailer. He was waiting for me and pointed to a chair for me to sit down. I started to tell him what June had requested of me in relation to killing the wolfman. John said that he already was aware of our conversation and had discussed it with his partners and they thought it would be a good deal. I asked him how he knew about our conversation. He said that June's trailer was equipped with very sensitive directional microphones. When June and I were talking in the corner of her apartment, they were tuned on and John heard almost every word that was said. John said that he thought it was a good plan and even though we had not thought of it as of yet. It was something that we should do. After all, we had to use every means possible to stop this predator. I agreed and shook my head yes. John said there would only be one change to the plan and that would be that I would have a partner on the advanced expedition. His name was Will Lynch. He was an older man who had been with John's group from the beginning. I didn't recognize his name, but John showed me his picture and I recognized him as one of the men aiding the investigation when I first met John at June's home. John thought I should reintroduce myself to him and get to know him better since we would be working together. John said, "It looks like you have four hours off in the rest trailer. I'll have one of the Suburbans drop you off there." He said that because our slowdown was for only five minutes and I had been talking to him longer than that.

I quickly got to the rest trailers. They were only about six miles behind the convoy. They look like big buses being towed by a tractor-trailer with a trailer hitch. I was told to take my pick because they were both outfitted about the same. It was still daytime, and no one was really sleeping; they were either watching TV, playing video games, or having coffee around the dining area. They quickly welcomed me when I went through the door. Everyone seemed to know my name and my story as to why I was part of the expedition. I felt like somewhat of a celebrity. They were very friendly, with that break the ice kind of talkativeness. But in a couple of minutes, they really got down to question me about what they really wanted to know. That was what they were really up against. They wanted to know what he looked like and how powerful he was. They had heard things, but I was the only one, besides June, who had lived to see him. I tried to fill the men in as best I could. They were truly amazed when I told them how he had jumped out of the tiger's den at the zoo, thirty feet out and twenty-five feet up. I was still amazed as I told them about it.

They had been told about June and her physical and mental capabilities. But they had no idea about her telepathic and mesmerizing powers. I thought it was best that I didn't mention it at this time. They also asked if I thought silver bullets would stop him. I told him that June had been tested with silver and that it had very detrimental effects on her. And since he was June's maker, we had to assume that silver bullets were a valuable weapon against him. They also asked if I thought he was possible to trap. I told them I didn't think it would ever happen. He was too smart, too fast, and too strong. I thought the only thing that would catch him was a bullet. They all kind of laughed and shook their heads yes.

Next, it was my turn to ask some questions. I asked them how long they had been in the program and how much training they had had. It appeared most had been in the program only three to four weeks. They were all from covert operations, black ops, and CIA programs. They had been training in these programs for some time. Their average commitment had been two to three years. At present, they were unassigned or waiting for an assignment. When this expedition came up, there were many interviews. They were told this was for only single men and women. They were also told this expedition had the possibility of being a oneway trip. They were told that their adversary was known to kill everyone and everybody who even knew of his existence. They were also told this was a hunt where the stakes were so high and the opponent so fierce that the hunters may not return. It was then that I saw the fear in their eyes. They had been hiding it well and it took a while for it to surface, but it was there in all of them, just like it was in me. They also related that during the interview they were told that they couldn't even tell that they were interviewed for this operation. This was a common procedure, and they didn't think too much of it. It was only when the few that were picked were told what the opponent was and that anyone that they had a conversation with about this opponent had a death sentence on their head. And then when they were filled in on how long he had been hunted, his victims, and how he had taken on a platoon of soldiers, they had started to become very anxious. The only good news that they had received in this deployment was that June, who was like the wolfman, could be sequestered and controlled. I didn't know if they were aware that our adversary could make a whole army of those like himself in just a couple of weeks. I thought it best not to mention it at this time. I looked around and saw that some of them were not wearing their sidearms. I told them I thought it was best that they had their sidearm with them always, 24/7, and that they should never be alone. They should always be in the largest group possible because when you consider his speed and strength, he's just too much for one person.

I just finished two cups of coffee with the men and women who were there and I told them I was going to get some rest. One of the men showed me through the door into the sleeping area. There are no windows or lights on, and it was very quiet. There were about twenty comfortable-looking bunks in that area. I selected one of the lower ones. They all had straps to secure you while you were sleeping, but I didn't feel like going up three tiers to the upper bunk. I had a little over two hours before I had to show up at my next station which was the lead Suburban. I needed to get a little rest. At least, that's what I thought I was going to do. But, instead, I had the most explosive wet dream of my life. Me and June, of course. I woke up in the middle of it all, sweating, panting, and throbbing. One of the guys a few bunks down from me asked if I was having a bad dream or something. I said yes and laid back down for a while. I was thinking that he thought I was some kind of nut case. I wondered if this was June's doing or just my imagination. It was so vivid and real, she had to cause some part of it in some way. I had only forty minutes until I was to report to my next station, so I turned off the alarm and took a shower and got ready.

My next station was the leading Suburban. It had three or four stations. Two operators were up front who were watching, listening, and receiving orders from the command center. The back of the Suburban had electronic surveillance equipment which ran scans on movement and body heat in any fast or abnormal movement in the area. I was stationed in the back, monitoring the surveillance equipment. On my way to my station, I noticed there were several .30 caliber automatic weapons hung on the walls that look like they were ready to be used at any time.

My station had been preprogrammed with alarms on all the equipment. If something was moving faster than expected, especially toward us, the alarm goes off on a screen and gives us the objects position. If there was a heat signature larger than a human's, an alarm would go off on that screen, also. Occasionally, you would see a person or animal walking near the road or an automobile. These would give off heat signatures and show up on the screen, but their importance was left up to the to me to decide if they were a threat. I had headphones on and a microphone so I could hear and speak to the people up front. They, on the other hand, had remote speakers and microphone so they could hear what was going on outside, also. Everything seemed to work pretty well. There were a couple of times when I had to tell them to get a visual on a cow or horse in a pasture. They would slow down and take a look with binoculars or a night viewer. I thought they must have been practicing a couple of days before I got there.

They were also in contact with their system to the mobile command center. I wasn't connected to that line. I only reported to the two men up front. My ability to alert the convoy was a little limited, I thought. But that was the way they wanted it. It was my understanding that the mobile command center had some of the same equipment. We were the forward observation group; a forward vanguard which they hope would pick up the movement first, and then they would back up our observations. I kind of felt like I was an expendable point man in this position.

But we did have the second Suburban watching us and backing this up. I knew, sooner or later, I would get to be stationed there and really find out what was going on in that position.

We were about to have our first supply and gas up. I was told the procedure for the positioning of the vehicles was as follows—the first Suburban was to go beyond the supply train; the second Suburban was to be on the outside, be it right or left on their flank; the supply train would be in between June's trailer, the mobile control center, and the second Suburban; and the last Suburban would be stationed thirty or forty feet away and watching the whole operation. Each of the Suburbans would position an outside man to cover their vehicles fueling and the fueling of the other vehicles. The supplies and food were hand-trucked to the designated vehicles. Once again, it all went so perfectly smooth that I was sure they had practiced the delivery operation for some time. I was also informed that the following trailers, where the other employees were resting, were supplied in the same fashion and that their own residents acted as the guards. I had only been at three stations and was learning an awful lot about this expeditionary adventure. My next station was going to be back at the mobile control center. There I could get something to eat, freshen up in the bathroom, and get to see what else was going on.

It was time for me to take another station at the mobile control center. Upon entering, I was told to be quiet because John was sleeping in an especially provided area where he could get rest and yet be available immediately. This time I was the liaison or go-between for the control center and all the other vehicles in the convoy. They all reported to me and I, in turn, communicated with each one of them, sometimes simultaneously, about what was happening. There was a very special connection to June's trailer which had priority above all other communications. Although I wasn't running the show, from this position, I got to see everything that was happening all at once. Since John wasn't there watching and controlling everything, I noticed the other employees appeared to want to be more communicative. Even though there was a lot of information coming to me from the other vehicles, I managed to talk to the other people for a while. Like the other soldiers in the resting trailer, they were very anxious to find out what we were up against. They flat out wanted to know if anyone ever killed one of these things. I told them that to the best of my knowledge no one ever had. But considering how secretive they are and how completely they cover their tracks, they must be afraid of us. I also told them like I told the other group to never go alone and always have their sidearm with them.

I asked what the procedure was to go to the bathroom and to get something to eat. I was informed that they were all trained already on my position and I just had to let them know I wanted to go, and someone would fill in. The coffee was on the counter by the refrigerator and food and beverages were in the refrigerator in the box next to it. Ed, who was standing near the radar unit, said that he would fill in for me. He didn't appear to be operating the unit by himself but was an extra man. After a visit to the head, I was very anxious to get involved with some food. There was all kinds of salads, sandwiches, sodas, and smoothies in the refrigerator. The box to it had an array of baked goods which all appeared to be fresh. Just as I was sitting down and getting ready to eat, John came out and grabbed some coffee. He told me that he had had no more than two or three hours' sleep at any one time for the past several days. He felt that sooner or later he would have to get some real sleep time in one of the rest trailers. I told him I didn't know how he did it because if I didn't get a good six or seven hours' sleep, I was always a little slower the next day. He said that he had been doing this all his life and that he knew his limits. Then he said for me not to be shy about asking any questions about procedures and workings at any of the stations I would be assigned. He said that most of the men and women had already been trained on all the stations. They pretty much knew what was supposed to be happening. John said, "You were the last person to be trained and that's because I wanted you to spend as much time as possible with June. These people have a little advanced training, and I'm sure you will be able to catch up very soon. But with you, you have a relationship with June that no one else has established."

I shook my head yes, knowing that I have a lot of learning to do in the next few days.

John said that he had invited Will Lynch over to the mobile center. He would arrive at the end of my shift. John wanted me to start to get to know the man. He said Will had been with him from the beginning. He was one of a few married men in our group. He said he had a wife and five children and that his dedication was outstanding. Besides being a good investigator, he had a sense for who we were pursuing. He was a big game hunter and knew how to track, stalk, post for any prey in the US. I told him I look forward to meeting him. John excused himself and went over to a couple of the other stations, and I finished my sandwich and went back to mine. Things were getting more and more exciting as we went along.

In a couple of hours, Will entered the control center. John motioned for me to come over to meet with them and for Ted to take over my position. His real name was William Lynch. He was just under six feet tall and what I would describe as a wiry built man. He looked thin, strong, and fast. He looked like he could walk through the woods all day. John introduced us, and then walked away. We sat down at one of the counters. William started right in, saying, "I understand we're going to be working together as an advanced scouting unit."

I said yes and shook my head. He asked, "What identifying features do we have of him?"

I said, "We have a possible video of a German-looking man in a baseball cap. He's tall, not too thin, and talks with a little German accent. We think he drives an older green Chevy Blazer. We have a few video stills from a hotel we know he was staying at. And, of course, on the night of the full moon, you'll immediately know him if you get to see it first."

Will said, "I'm prepared for that with my .50 caliber Win Mag." Smiling assuredly, he said, "We've estimated that at that time of the month, he is seven to eight feet tall and weighs around 800 pounds. He's about the size of a large grizzly bear but more than twice as powerful. I look forward to facing him at that time."

I shook my head yes and said, "That's what I remember seeing. I also said that he has a lot of speed, not to mention a superior intelligence and cunning."

Will said, "Yes, that's what I find so attractive and engaging in our quest. We are going up against one who is smarter and stronger than we are."

I asked him, "Does that scare you at all?"

He said, "Of course. But hunting is a science, and if you use the proper procedure and guards, you will have a good chance of success. Of course, there are always unforeseen circumstances. But that is what makes it so exciting."

I shook my head like I agreed but I was not sure this was my way of looking at the pursuit of the killer. I wanted to get to him and kill him because he was a murderous fiend who was too quick and strong to be captured. I would be saving many lives, along with June's and probably my own. There would be no joy, sense of accomplishment, or pride in the kill for me. I was just riding this world of this terrible disease. I really didn't care what Will's personal motivation was. I just wanted to end this trail of horror.

Just as we were finishing up, John came over and reported that one of the lieutenants who was overseeing June's incarceration had been found killed in his apartment. It has happened a few days ago but it was just discovered this morning when he didn't report to work. All initial indications pointed to our wolfman. This assumption was arrived at because of the condition of the body. Our department was taking over the investigation and our men were over there at present taking pictures, DNA samples, and figuring out how this happened. I asked John what the man's name was. He said he was Lt. John Sand. I immediately remembered he was the one who June was flirting with at his desk when I had come in once. I thought this was very significant and asked John to speak to me privately about this. It appeared the people at risk from our overall operation had increased considerably.

John and I went over to a corner of the control unit, and I told him about how June had been flirting with the lieutenant, about how she was out of her apartment, and leaning on the lieutenant's desk and talking to him in a very flirtatious way. I had observed this several times but have failed to mention it. I also told John that the reasons I failed to mention it were somewhere between the fact that I was a little jealous and that I could not determine if this was insignificant or part of June's mesmerizing.

John said, "At this point, I think we can surmise that it might have meant something to someone or something." John looked me straight in the face and said, "You have to learn to trust me and the people in our department. Whatever it is, no matter how embarrassing, no matter how belittling, make sure you let us know what is going on. Our adversary will take advantage of our human weakness, our hate, envy, our desire for revenge, and even our love to overcome us. The only way that we can beat him is to share all of our humanity with each other—the good, the bad, and even the indifference. Humanity is something he does not possess. It is something that we have over him. When our relationships are strong, we are strong. He cannot overcome us then. It is only when we go off on our own into ourselves, our own self-absorption that he has a chance."

All of a sudden, I had tears in my eyes. I could see the truth. Also, I knew and could see why John was the head of our department. He knows who we are, and he knows how we are at our best. I was drying the tears from my eyes and shaking my head that I understood. Then John said, "If I had known what you have told me just now, I would've removed that young man from the position. There is a general rule that there is to be no camaraderie between June and her guards. As you know, this rule does not apply to you. You are encouraged to establish and maintain as deep a relationship with June as much as possible."

I said, "I understand."

It was time for my next station which was the small control area in the cab of the tractor-trailer which was pulling June's residential area trailer. I passed Will on the way over and he said that he was stationed in the control booth at the end of June's trailer. Coincidentally, we would be stationed in areas fronting and backing June. The cab area was very small, probably no more than eight by eight feet. Three men could fit in the area, but with only two, it could be comfortable. It was the back cab of the tractor-trailer. Most of them are made out of fiberglass, but this one was steel reinforced with large plates of steel all around. We were in direct contact with all the other vehicles. All the input from other vehicles came into speakers mounted in the front and back. Our main job was to receive information and transport the wolf girl, as they called her. The defensive weaponry was standard machine guns, rifles, and hand grenades. An interesting addition was an array of rocket launchers positioned on the back of the cab. They contained silver nitrate crystals and gas. They were multidirectional and could be aimed anywhere from ten feet to one hundred yards. We had one override, and that was from the control booth in June's trailer. They could stop us at any time by just flipping a switch. This was probably a safety precaution in case they could see something we couldn't see.

Me and Leo were in the cab. Our job was to monitor and report on the video from to cameras with wide-angle lenses which focused about 45-degree posterior. We also supported the two men up front in any way they needed. There were windows with holes to shoot out of just underneath the window. These were on all four walls and gave the views of the top of June's trailer, the top of the tractor-trailer, and both sides of the cab. I asked the men how long they were training in this station, and they said it was about a month. They said they were training in a mockup construction even before this whole vehicular unit was put together.

They told me that they were instructed to make sure I was able to handle all the stations, including driving. This was going to be a little challenging since I had never driven a tractor-trailer before and with such a heavy load. They turned out to be excellent instructors, and it was easier than I thought when I found out that the transmission was automatic. I ended up driving for about an hour and half. It was all on wide highways. The person next to me supported me with the GPS as to what lane I should be in and how fast I should be going. I found it kind of enjoyable driving such a big rig. I was surprised at the amount of horsepower that the engine had. If you stepped on it, it would automatically downshift and really take off. You would get G forces pushing you hard against the back of your seat. It was a real rush of adrenaline. Well, it was time to slow down and get into my next station.

Surprisingly enough, my next station was in the control booth of June's residential trailer. Again, I passed Will because he was taking my previous position. At this station, I would be monitoring June for about three hours. I didn't mind doing this at all. As a matter of fact, I enjoyed seeing her. She just flowed as she moved around the apartment. She was always doing something, never sitting quiet and pensive. She really kept the matron very busy watching her. The only drawback was that I could not interact with her.

The booth was specifically designed for totally monitoring June. There were video recorders and microphones all over June's apartment. We could hear and see everything she was doing, and it was recorded. It was hard to know exactly everything she was doing and why. Sometimes she would be looking up things on the computer. Then she would run over and look some information up in a book, then take some notes, and then back to the computer. She was a very busy girl. All this time, she was getting feedback from the air we were passing through. Her own living room air was being filtered and scrubbed before it was let back into the environment. So far, we had had no hits, meaning she hadn't picked up the scent. We were all waiting for that to happen.

Suddenly, we got a direct message from John. Satellite imagery had picked up an older green Chevy Blazer similar to the one we were searching for. It was seen several hundred miles from us and much further North than we were headed. Since this was our only lead, John said we were going up that way to check it out. I figured it was a one in 1,000 chance it would be our guy. But if you are just driving around, searching, going North is just as good. I thought it was the right call. I checked the GPS and found that we were headed into a less populated area. Roads were not as well traveled and not as wide. There were a few towns between large areas of wilderness. In such an area, it would be harder to hide in plain sight as in a large city. But the wilderness, this would provide many escape routes. I thought that now we were going into a territory that would be more favorable to his aptitudes and skills.

John called me and said that just in case we had a contact, he wanted me to be briefed on how Will and I would operate. He set up a meeting with me and Will, so I could be filled in on what to expect and how we should operate. When a contact was initiated and a direction established, we were to go to the nearest town and rent a couple of cars. From there, we would proceed well ahead— fifty to one hundred miles ahead of the convoy—and then come back searching and hoping to run into him. While in our individual cars, Will and I would be in direct contact with each other with a couple of walkie-talkies with headphones for hands-free operation. They were supposed to have a range over thirty miles, although we were told never to become separated by more than ten miles. What we would be doing was being mobile posts hoping to spot or run into the killer. Each of us would have a knapsack filled with supplies which included food and water, rifle and ammunition, night goggles, of course, a GPS, motion detector, and a chemical spray to reduce our scent. We didn't need any instruction on how to use the supplies since we had been using them already. I had initially thought that Will and I would be in the same vehicle, but by being in two different cars, we could search a lot more area. This did make it a little more frightening since backup was not right next to you. I would have to be a lot more observant and aware of what was going on around me.

Will also told me that once we think we've made a positive contact, we are to inform and then wait for our partner. There is no way that we should take on this guy on our own. I mentioned to Will that there were no handcuffs or tranquilizers in our bags. He looked at me and said, "We are just going to kill him."

I kind of already knew that and was just checking for certainty. There was a short pause and Will asked, "Any questions or anything else you feel you might need?"

I said, "No."

Then he said, "Okay, let's get back to our stations."

I had a couple of hours to spend in the last vehicle of the convoy. Like the other Suburbans, it was black with tinted windows. It had armaments and surveillance equipment but most striking was the multi-barreled machine gun unit which at a moment's notice would pop up through the roof. It had a 360-degree rotation capability. I was told that because we were guarding the rear, we had a view of the whole convoy. Any attack to any of the other vehicles, we were to pull up and engage the attackers. If we were attacked from our rear or either of our flanks, we were to hold our position, fight, and notify control what was going on. That seems simple enough, but what wasn't simple was all the ammunition stored throughout the vehicle. Apparently, this machine gun fired a lot of ammunition very quickly. I heard it was over 3,000 rounds a minute, and if they were all silver bullets, it would be a very expensive gun to fire.

There were four of us in the Suburban. Two up front and two in the back. I was monitoring the radar equipment for any unusual movement and viewing the wide-angle video from the posterior cameras. The driver continually swerved right and left so he could view both sides of the convoy. The guy with me in the back was a real gun head. All he did was polish, oil, and play with his six-barreled machine gun. He didn't say much; he was just kind of all over the gun. I asked him how long he had been training with the weapon. He said that he been with her a little over a month. I knew he really loved that gun.

The other two men were quite talkative. They both come from the CIA. They both specialized in combat defensive driving. They like doing what they were doing. They had some questions about June, like who she was and what she looked like before and during the full moon. I told them that I never saw her during her full moon phase but otherwise she was an attractive-looking woman. Then they asked about the other wolfman. They said that they heard he was big and mean. I told them he was big and fast and more mean than they could imagine. One of them said, "That's hard for me to imagine."

I said, "That's what I just said, and I hope you don't have to find out what he's capable of."

It was time for me to go back to the mobile control vehicle. We were also having a supply and refill stop. As I was entering the mobile center, John was exiting. He said he was going back to the rest trailer to get some real sleep. The supply unit was going to drop him off with the rest of the people who were scheduled for rest. My job was working with Art who was taking John's place for the time being. They wanted me to get an overall view of the whole operation and how it was orchestrated. It appeared we were running the show, but there was a standing order that if anything happened that was significant, John was to be immediately notified. In reality, John was still there with us, running the program as he had been from the beginning.

Art, who had been with John from the beginning and who I remembered when I first came into the program, appeared to have a lot of questions. They weren't so much about what happened and how I got in the program but they were more about what I felt about it, what I thought about my situation, and what I thought all this meant. I thought he was a lot into drama rather than facts and solutions. He did, however, caused me to think about things in a different way. So it was an interesting and informative conversation. Maybe this is why John has Art on the team. He sees things a little differently.

It was the end of the shift, and we got what we were waiting for. June reported a faint scent of our wolfman. We notified John and he had us go into our directional determination procedure. In this procedure, we would drive around in increasingly larger concentric circles to where we first got his scent. The scent levels would be plotted as we drove around. We would take note of the high scent areas and see if we could extrapolate a direction that he was traveling. Once that was clearly established, the convoy would head off in that direction. Will and I would also spring forward on our mission, and we would try to catch him in between. This direct channel determination procedure was going to take between five and six hours. We called for a supply and gas up stop because we did not know what kind of territory we would be going into and we wanted to have adequate supplies to finish the procedure. Everyone was excited. You can see an increased determination and focus in their movements and speech. Things were moving faster, literally.

I thought to myself, *Here we are. Around two days out and we already get a hit. I couldn't have planned it better myself, or were we in somebody else's plan?* In this thing, I wondered, are we the pursuer or the follower? Are we the hunters or just controlled pawns being used for some unknown reason? The big question is and always has been, where does the trail of the wolf lead? I didn't have an answer for that question. Too many things had happened. I had invested so much in this pursuit. There was so much loss along the way. I had paid to be here. I had made a choice at some point. A choice where I didn't know the total cost and still don't know. A choice where I didn't know how much time it would take and still don't know. A choice where I didn't know the outcome and still don't know.

Why would anyone make such a choice? I had to be out of my mind. What was so enticing? Who was I trying to be? A good person? I was a good person with my family and my job as a professor. A destroyer of evil? All I've seen is his passion for destruction and killing. I haven't stopped him at all. All I've really done is wade through his trail of guts of slaughtered people, half eaten children, and machinations of superhuman control with an ego that appears to be insatiable.

And here I am. I feel like I'm being pulled through all of this. I'm out of control, in a way, because I can't quit. Something in me has to go on to the end of this thing, whatever it might be. I can't think of any word in the English language that really defines my position right now. I think it's somewhere between committed and condemned.

Well, it finally happened. We got a direction of the scent trail. It was totally Northeast on all the calculations. Will and I were already packed and ready to go. The largest town where we could pick up some rental cars was called Muscatine. From there, we would spring forward to Marshalltown and start searching backward. I looked at the map and it was a lot of ground to cover. I thought it would take us nearly a week to cover all the towns along the way. But since John wanted us to work together, we were looking at even more time on the road. Just as we were getting into the Suburban to take us for our rentals, John reminded us of what we were looking for. It was an older Chevy Blazer, green, with a special make of tire. He also said that every hour we should both check in as to where we were.

It took us about forty-five minutes to get to Muscatine. John's people had already reserved a couple of cars for us at a rental agency. We had an SUV and a large family sedan waiting for us. All the arrangements had been made in the way of financing and rental time. We just had to get our things into the cars and leave right away for Marshalltown. Will said that he preferred to have the SUV. That was okay with me since it was very large and looked like it would get poor gas mileage. My car had a large trunk and plenty of seating in the front and back. It was a large luxury sedan which probably be more comfortable to drive. The large trunk was useful in keeping the equipment and many of the firearms out of sight.

We took off traveling as fast as we could. We were speeding pretty fast since we had to make up about 150 miles before we started our search. About an hour or so into our drive, I noticed a state trooper's car with its lights flashing. Obviously, he wanted us to pull over. I notified Will on the walkie-talkie, and we both pulled over to the shoulder. It occurred to me at that moment that this could get very sticky if he asked to search our cars and found all the firepower we were carrying. I thought it was very important we tell him right up front that we were federal agents working an investigation. After checking our credentials, the trooper said he still wanted to call his captain since it was usual procedure to notify the authorities of any investigations or deployments in the area. I told him there was a special number on the back of my ID which the captain could call to verify our operation. With that, he went back to his patrol car and stayed on the microphone for about five minutes. When he came back, he said that we were cleared to go and that the troopers up ahead were notified that we were on our way and not to bother us. We took our credentials back, smiled, said thank you, and quickly left.

It was dark by the time we got to Marshalltown, so we decided to take a hotel for the night. We got up early and started canvassing all the motel areas. Since he was on the move, we thought that he would not be staying in a residential area. Most of our work was main streets and highways. Then it was on to the next town and the town after that and the town after that.

In two days, we met John coming up in one of the highways. Since he was still on the scent trail and it was increasingly strong, we were ordered to go out another 250 miles Northeast. John told us that this was only our first try. Since the scent window is only about one hundred miles, there's a good chance that we passed him on the way down. It appears he is still on the move so we will have to do this procedure again. He said, "You will have to keep searching. Sooner or later, you will catch him or he will stop, and the expedition will catch up to him. We have to do this before he discovers what we are doing. If he does, he may mask his scent and/or change direction and run."

Will and I said we understood.

I asked, "Could we get a good meal and a couple of hours' rest before we left?"

John said, "Okay."

It was dark already when we left. We had four to five hours of driving ahead of us. The countryside was becoming less populated as we drove Northeast. When we got to the 250-mile mark, there were no hotels or motels, and we had to drive another fifty miles to find lodging. We had to get a good night's sleep because the next couple of days would entail a lot of driving and searching. The next day and a half, we were occupied doing the same procedure. We drove up and down the streets in the residential and commercial areas, looking for a green Chevy Blazer or any suspicious signs.

Once again, we found ourselves near John's approaching expeditionary force. When we were about twenty miles from him, he told us to turn around and go out another 300 miles in the same direction, Northeast. So we turned around, got some gas and food, and took off again. This time, it was forty to fifty miles in between each town and the towns were a lot smaller. We both thought it would be easier searching for him in the smaller town. Once again, when we got to the 300-mile mark, there were no places to lodge. We found a place on the GPS, but it was fifty miles offtrack. We were tired and we took it, anyway.

The next town in the Northeast search was Pencer. To get to the town, we had to travel West to go around a national park. It was a little town resting near the Northwestern part of the park. When we got there, we discovered the town was smaller than it looked on the map. It was going to take us three to four hours tops to cover the whole town completely. I took the Eastern part near the state park, and Will took the Western half. In most towns in the sparse areas, the majority of the residents live outside of town anywhere from two to ten miles. The homes were sparsely located but very easy to check out. Will and I agreed to save the center of town for last. That way, we would be able to get something to eat together. About two and a half hours later, I told Will I would be starting to check out the outskirts of the town. He let me know he was almost there himself.

This was a small town with very few tall buildings. There were fifteen streets running East to West and ten streets running North to East. There would be no more than an hour or two hours' work for both of us. The Northeast portion of this town was the most rundown. There were a few sleazy hotels, bars, pool rooms, and mom and dad eateries. There was a fair number of cars parked on the street and a lot of people hanging around. I didn't think this was the place where our wolfman could be hiding. Oh my, was I wrong. Right in front of one of those sleazy hotels was the green Blazer I had been searching for. I parked down the street and walked up and checked the tires. They were the same ones for which we had been looking. Everything was a match so far. I walked up to the front of the hotel and looked in on one of the large glass windows where I could observe the lobby and reception desk. There were three or four couches and three or four stuffed chairs in the lobby which were all unoccupied. The place was old and dusty and rundown. It had the decor of the 1940s. It looks like only derelicts and the lowest caste of society would reside there. There was a young fellow in his twenties sitting at the reception desk watching television. He turned around and smiled at me when I walked into the lobby.

I walked up to the young man at the desk and said, "Hello." He said, "Hi" back. I couldn't help but notice he was very clean cut. He looked like he didn't come from this neighborhood. He looked like he might be a college kid working his way through college. There were a stack of newspapers and a register on the counter/desk. He turned around in his chair and rested his elbows on the counter. He asked, "How can I help you?"

I remarked that he had a nice little town here and that it seemed very quaint and quiet. He said, "It is quiet, that's for sure. There's never anything going on around here."

I asked if he knew the person who owned the green Blazer out front. He said it belongs to the owner of the hotel. I asked if he knew where I could find him. He said, "If he's home, he is up on the third floor. He has his own entrance around the back, so he wouldn't know if he was in or not." I asked how I could get up to the third floor, and he said that I would have to take the stairs, while pointing over to the corner of the room. He volunteered that I could take the elevator to the second floor, but to get to the third floor, I would have to walk up the stairs because the elevator only went to the second floor. He also said that I wouldn't have any trouble finding the owner on the third floor because he occupied the entire third floor as his home. Right then, looking at the size of the hotel, I thought to myself he must have 3,000 square feet of living space up there. I thanked the young man and walked over to the stairs and started going up. I didn't see anyone at all on the stairwell and was glad of that because I didn't have a very good description of the person I was looking for. If I passed him on the stairs, I might not recognize him. I thought it wise to be as quiet as possible on the last set of stairs. But from what June had been telling me about their hearing and smelling abilities, he would probably already know I was here.

When I got to the top of the third flight of stairs, I could hear music from a record player coming from an open door about halfway down the hall. I was walking down the hall toward the door with my gun drawn. I couldn't help but notice the 1950s vintage old linoleum flooring. Just then, I remembered that I had not notified Will of my discovery and that we were overdue for our hourly check-in. Plus, John had ordered us to have backup if we approach this guy. I pulled out my walkie-talkie and clicked the send button and began to talk. I was surprised to hear a click and my voice on a walkie-talkie coming from inside the room of the open door. I thought, *Could Will be here already?* I quickly jumped into the open doorway with my gun outstretched in my hands in front of me.

There was a man sitting in an old-fashioned stuffed chair with his right side facing me about twenty feet away from me. There was an old-fashioned record player playing a stack of 78 records about 15 feet in front of him. The room was dim. There was one large lamp on the table with record player and a small reading lamp on a table next to the stuffed chair where the man was sitting. He looked at me and waved me, saying, "Come on in. I've been waiting for you."

I immediately said, "Where's Will? I hear his walkie-talkie."

The man looked at me and said, "I met your friend about twenty minutes ago and he will not be joining us."

I moved a little closer to him and cocked the hammer of my .44 Magnum. I was getting ready to shoot him. He put his hand up as if to say stop and said, "Please I have so much to tell you, about why and how you are here. There is so much I'm sure you want to know. And I also have something for you. Something of great value. Please have a seat over by the record player. It won't hurt you if we just talked a while. Also, please turn off the record player. No one will bother us up here."

I thought, *This guy is about to get blasted and he is giving orders?* I don't know why I didn't pull the trigger then. I knew I was extremely curious, and it appeared I was in control. I said that I preferred not to sit but I did take a position over by the record player where I could look at him head-on.

He was similar to what we had thought he would be. A lanky yet muscular man about six-two to six-three feet tall. He looked to be of German descent with short hair and he was starting to go bald. He talked with a slight German accent and was smiling as he talked. "Well," he said. "It did take you some time for you to get here. *I* had been expecting you for a while. I'm sure June helped you in some ways, also."

I immediately blurted out, "What do you know about June?"

He said, "I know a lot about her. I made her the way she is. She is my prodigy."

Then I asked, "Do you mean you did that to her on purpose?"

He leaned forward and said, "Yes."

This sounded strange and almost unbelievable because I thought June was lucky to have escaped alive. I had assumed that she was supposed to be killed with the rest of her family and that at some point he wanted to finish the job because her just being alive gave us too much information about the type of creature he was. I was a little stunned and just stood there.

Right away, he continued, "You know I have been following you for some time? It was ever since I saw you and June walking to her parents' house. You see, I had spent many years searching for the right genetic makeup and *I* had found it in June, and then there you were walking with her the same day I freed her from her family, another genetically suitable human. What a coincidence. What a gift."

I was really shocked by his statements mainly because it was me and my team following him. And he didn't free June from anything; he imprisoned her for the rest of her life in a well-guarded apartment. I was going to tell him what was in my mind, but he quickly went on.

"Once I discovered you, I had to bring you to me unhindered and free to make the choice of your life." He sat up and leaned toward me and said, "You notice I never touched your family. They are being taken care of by a good man who will take care of them and will not leave them."

I was really pissed off when I heard that and I quickly blurted out, "How do you know that's true?"

He said, "You have much to learn, but we have our ways of instigating things."

I kind of took that as his admittance to causing my divorce.

He kept going, saying, "You have been following my trail and you think you have been learning about me. Actually, I have been learning about you. I have been grooming you for this day. As you have been following me, you have been divesting yourself of many of your human cares. I have become your main focus in life. For whatever reason you may have had in your mind to come here today, I have had a reason in my mind to bring you here today as you are. Your following my trail has changed you, and I think you know that to be true. The leader of your team, John, in some ways, is like you. He has no life, no interest outside of pursuing me. I have become the wellspring of his life. When I go into action, he finally becomes alive. I'm his reason for living. But you, Jordan, have so much more potential."

I said, "Exactly what do you mean?"

He said, "I will get to that very soon. First, I want to tell you about something I have for you and a little bit about myself."

All this time he was talking, I was thinking this guy is really full of himself. But now it sounds like he wants to spill his guts to me. So I thought, *Why not?* I am standing about twelve feet from him. I have a .44 Magnum with silver bullets pointed at his heart. My gun is pointed at him, and I think I can pull the trigger and about a tenth of a second. I think I'll take a chair and sit down and listen. So I sat down and said, "Go on."

He went on, "You probably don't know it, but I am over 250 years old. I was the son of a nobleman who was attacked by a were-wolf while I was returning from visiting a young maiden. My guards and I tried to fight, but they were quickly killed along with their horses. I was bitten but only survived because my horse kicked him away and took off running with me on board. He was a magnificent steed and was able to outrun the werewolf at the start. I don't know why, but the wolf gave up the chase. He could have easily caught up to us, but for some reason, I was spared death.

"When I got back to my father's palace and told them what happened, they immediately understood and built a caged area in what used to be a torture chamber. My parents protected me for almost thirty years. After their demise, it was trusted servants who took care of me. I found that I would have to move to different places where I was not known every thirty or forty years. The reason was that I aged very slowly. At the age of one hundred, I still look to be in my thirties. The whole time up to about 130 years of age, I never hurt anyone. My life was well planned and orchestrated. This was aided by the fact that the gift gave me increased intellect and strength. I amassed a tremendous amount of wealth. I even tried marriage and had a child. It ended badly when my wife could no longer stand having a wolf baby. She consulted the church, and they killed her and the child—her for being a witch and the child for being a demon. Then I was forced to leave the country."

"After that, I became disenchanted with humanity. I let myself run free with the full moon. I embraced who I was and endeavored to become a better and more powerful me. I made others like myself, but they acted poorly and caused much trouble and chaos. They could not handle the power and were often killing out in the open. I ended up having to destroy them all."

"I discovered that there were other ones like myself. They were older and smarter and stayed secluded. They built layers of protection and supportive people around themselves. There happens to be seven of these werewolves, including myself, living in the United States today. They are all older and stronger than I am. They are very territorial and do not like to mix company. For that reason, I am relegated to this general area of the country. So, you see, of my race, I am considered the most insignificant and least important. But I am endeavoring to change that."

And I said to him, "With all your talents and strength, why don't you try to help humanity and make the world a better place?"

He said, "Your humanity is so flawed and so self-absorbed, the only ones they want to help are themselves and at that to the expense of others. Your humanity only does good when there's something in it for them. Of course, your leaders are such liars about how magnanimous they are, about how they are doing this or that for humanity. All they are doing is putting themselves in a better and more powerful position. From imperfect flawed people, you get imperfect flawed actions. And don't expect anything from the government because the government is made of the same imperfect flawed people."

Then he looked at me and leaned forward and said, "So you expect something different from my kind. We are part human and we carry the same flaws. Only with our potential we can take chaos and destruction to a level of which you will never be capable. I find me as one who finds it best to just stay out of your affairs. That is till I discovered June."

I quickly asked, "What is it about June?"

He said, "I'm going to get to that, but first let me tell you what I have for you." He turned in his seat and pointed with his left hand over to the corner of the room. He said, "See those files there?"

I said, "Yes."

He continued, "There are eight financial firms that have accounts already in your name. A total of around $155 million dollars."

I looked at him with a puzzled face and said, "I don't quite understand. Why me?"

He said, "In a very short time, you will understand. In addition to those files in the corner," he said, pointing to the opposite side of the room. "There are about $300 million dollars in accounts where you have ownership as a survivor."

I was so stunned. All I can say is, "But why?"

He quickly changed the subject and asked, "What do you think of June?"

I said, "I think she's a very beautiful and smart woman."

He then said, "You know werewolf women are the most alluring creatures in the world to human men. No man can deny them. Wherever June is at present, she is there because she wants to be there. I picked June because her genetics signaled that she would be a powerful, intelligent, and even devoted wolf mother."

I stood up and said, "That's it! You want to mate with June because that's the only way to get a more powerful werewolf—to have two werewolves mate."

He looked at me very inquisitively and asked, "How do you know that?"

For some reason, I felt very compelled to tell him and I said, "The wolfman from New Orleans told me."

Then he said, "Well, you know a little more than I thought you knew." Incidentally, he said, "That werewolf's got himself in a sweet spot. He never has to leave his compound, and he gets everything he needs handed to him on a platter. Those people love him and will never give him up."

And I said, "You're right. He's the only thing that's keeping them going right now."

He smiled and shook his head yes.

I asked him, "How do I fit into all of this?"

He said, "I will show you." He held out his left hand palm up and said, "To see the truth, you must look deeply into my hand. You must concentrate and watch it change. You don't have to come any closer. My hand will not hurt you. In it, you will see truth. You will see your life and your future. You don't have to move. You need only look."

I looked at his outstretched left hand. It looked like it had waves of light emanating from its center. The skin texture was changing and his nails were extending out into claws. His hand was getting larger, maybe two to three times its size. All the while, his hand was glowing with a yellowish kind of glow, with darker waves of brown and yellow emanating out from its center. I had never seen anything like it. It was mesmerizing. I don't know how long I was looking at his hand, but the thought of being mesmerized caused me to quickly look up at the rest of him. The rest of the him had been changing along with his hand. And by time I looked up, his hand that was supposed to be extended out to me was hanging at his side and he was already moving toward me ever so fast.

I managed to get a shot off, just as his teeth bit into my left shoulder at the root of my neck. He immediately fell back into the chair that he had been sitting on and was bent over, holding his left side. He raised his right hand, pleading, "Don't shoot! Don't shoot! This was necessary, and now you will understand. More and more each day, you will understand how much of a gift I have given you. You will be much better than me, stronger, smarter. You have a kinder heart than me. There is something more you have to know."

I was hit fast and hard. He moved a lot faster than I ever thought he could. I was surprised and stunned. The only thing that pushed him back was my shot into his left side. He was talking and raising his hand. I could hear his words and knew the verbiage, but I really didn't know what it truly meant for me. With my pistol pointed at him still, I fell back into the chair. The pain in my shoulder pulsed all through my body. It was a lot more severe than I had expected for the bite that I had received. I wanted to shoot him again, but something in me caused me to hold back. I was infected and was afraid. He was telling me things about myself. I wanted desperately to know what was going on. It seemed the only one who could help me now was my attacker.

He quickly went on to say, "You're going to be all right. It was just a little bite. It won't be fatal. I know you're afraid, but please relax. You are going to be so much better. It will be several months before you completely mature. You should go see June. She will immediately know what happened as soon as you get near her. She will tend to you and help you along. Since she has been through this herself, she will guide you. You will have to start making certain changes in your life, but don't worry because you will be smarter and more capable as time goes on."

I was dazed. I could barely understand what he was saying. Now, instead of two werewolves to deal with, there were going to be three, and I was going to be one of them. I said, "I don't understand. What's going on? Why me?"

As I said that, I was looking at him. He was half man and half beast. For some reason, he had stopped changing. He had grown much taller and his body was becoming covered with hair. His head was now partially canine, with his snout displaying two-inch canine teeth. His body dimensions had increased in size, also. He was just bigger, with a lot more muscle. His hands had increased about three times their size, with two-inch claws projecting from his fingers. He was still holding his left side with his left hand. Then he pointed his right finger at me and said, "You… You thought that I want to mate with June. You were wrong. It's you who is for June. With your and June's genetic types, you will have a superior wolf child. It will be stronger, smarter, and more capable than any of our kind before it. You told me you wanted to help humanity. Do it. You want to benefit humanity. Do it. If you want to lead humanity to a better place, you can do that to. I have given you and June everything you need to start. Once you and her become a pair, you won't need me anymore. I am your maker, but not your leader. I consider you both superior to me, and your child will be the best."

He continued to say, "I have to strongly caution you. Do not tell anyone what has happened, especially the people you work for. They will not see your philanthropic side. I am sure they will immediately lock you up far away from June. And if they really find out what's going on, they will destroy one or both of you. They won't want your help. From the beginning, humanity has failed to listen, even to God. What makes you think that they will want to listen to you? Anything you do with them, you will have to do covertly so they don't know it's you doing it. But you will learn much about this later."

Then he smiled a most monstrous wicked smile. He said then, "After all, you may decide like I did that they are too stubborn and not worth your time. You may find it more exhilarating to be a predator and a hunter, selecting and pursuing your prey. I can tell you there is nothing more intoxicating for a wolf or a man than being the hunter of men. You will find it most exhilarating, the taking down of humans who think they are at the top of the food chain. Once you do that and taste their blood, you will never be able to go back. I would love to hunt with you and June. There is so much I could teach you. There is so much you could learn from me about a whole new level of existence."

I was emotionally stunned. This asshole is just a killer. Why was he telling me this? Was this a test? What was he trying to find out? It didn't matter because his suggestion was so obnoxious to me; so threatening to everything that I hold sacred as a human and a physician. With great anger and angst, I pulled the trigger and shot him in the mouth. He fell back in his chair with his head facing the ceiling. Then as I looked at him sitting there, I realized why I had to kill him. Even though the things he was saying were terrible and obnoxious, there was a certain attractiveness to his statements. It was the attractiveness of having power over others; the use of skill and cunning to

conquer your prey. It was a game of death. And I didn't ever want to have him convince me to go there. So I had to end it.

This part was over, and he was right. There was something rewarding about finally taking down your prey, especially one like him. But from what he said, I was the main object of the hunt. I was the prey and I was very puzzled. Did he win? Did he capture me? Did he orchestrate his own death or did I kill him of my own accord? Now there were more questions in my head than answers. What was I to do? He told me not to trust anyone. I could tell John and hope he believes that I will be of benefit to society from my cage that he will probably put me in. And then there is always the chance that they will want to exterminate me, especially if he finds out that there are eight of us now in this country. And what does June expect? Then I thought, *Oh God, how did I get myself into this?* It's amazing that people never consult God when they're going into something. It is only when things don't work out or they are in trouble that they start to look up, asking for help. Right now, I thought it best that I should touch base with June before I did anything. After all, she is smarter than all of us and probably knows more about God than anyone and would have an insight beyond mine as to what I should do.

Right now, there were more pressing things. I had to dispose of or store the body. I thought I could wrap it in several layers of plastic. That would secure it for a few days after which I could bury it or store it in a freezer. Either way, it would probably be months before he was missed. Then there was the problem of the financial records. They wouldn't be safe where they were at present. I thought I should put them in a storage facility until I could figure out exactly what to do about them. Since I was supposed to be headed back to see John, I had to get moving on these two projects.

With a little searching, I found the keys for the Blazer and parked it around the back where no one would see me carrying down the financial records. I found a storage facility and parked the car with the records inside in a large storage rental space. I took a cab back to my car and picked up ten rolls of duct tape, several large plastic bags used for construction debris, and four large and thick painter's drop cloths. All this took me about two and a half hours. It was only about half an hour to wrap the body in about five or six layers of plastic. It would be some time before the odor would start to leak out, but by that time, I would have been able to dispose of it. I slipped the body over to a corner where the financial records were and covered it with several comforters and pillows. After cleaning up all the blood, I found the keys and locked the door on my way out.

Even though I was still in shock and pain from what had happened, I was still able to go through the motions required for the cleanup. I thought. I have a plan and I'm going to work the plan and not think about anything else for now. But after all the work was done and I was driving back to see John and talk to June, I started to realize some of the implications of what had happened in the past few hours. I realized that I was in big trouble and I had very few options. I can go back and tell everything to John, throwing myself totally under his control. The best I can hope for was living in a caged apartment like June. But I don't think they would let me stay there for 300 or 400 years or as long as I could live. The more I drove back to the convoy the less appealing this option seemed.

Another thing I could do was just take the money and run. Without the proper support of trusted people, it will be extremely difficult. And if I don't show up, John will suspect sooner or later what had happened and then he would be on my trail. Also, there's the possibility that this action would put June at risk and I didn't want to do that. So the more I drove the clearer it became that my best chance of survival would be if somehow I could team up with June. How this would play out was completely unimaginable, yet I know it was the best chance that I would have. And it was becoming clearer and clearer to me that this was all planned for, orchestrated by, and implemented by the wolfman that I had just killed.

He had trapped me and not put me to death but put me in the life I didn't want. I had wondered where his trail would lead; now I know. Now his trail had become my trail. For some reason, I thought of the twenty-third Psalm which ended in the statement, "May goodness and mercy follow me all the days of my life and I will dwell in the house of the Lord forever." I wondered what kind of trail I would leave. Would it be goodness and mercy or destruction and death?

The wolfman told me that he had lived the first hundred years or so without hurting anyone and that he became disillusioned with humanity. I was already feeling disillusioned with humanity and not trusting them very much. I wondered if I had it in me to go one hundred years without hurting humans.

It was with the very best intentions that I started this hunt. I had wanted to stop a merciless predator from killing innocent men, women, and children. I see now that I was led along. I gave up so much. What was this evil that caused me to leave my good life behind? How did evil mask itself as something so good and beneficial to mankind, and why was I so attracted to it? My mind was overwhelmed with such questions, and the answers were somewhere beyond my understanding, if they even existed at all. One thing that I did know for sure is that the end of this hunt is the beginning of another, and that the hunter is now the hunted. The trail of the wolf continues.

Suffix

Well, it was quite a journey. I'm glad we made it through together. Thank you for coming along. It looks like Dr. Blaine is not the same as when he started. And to tell you the truth, I'm not the same, either. And if there's been a change in you, I hope it's for the better. There were some really hard places for Dr. Blaine to get through. I think he did the very best he could, considering what and who he was up against. If it were me in his position, I don't think I could've done as well as him.

I am amazed at how easily we humans can be pulled away from the preeminent things of value and worth in our lives to go after something else. Not that the thing we were going after it is bad, it's just something good taking the place of something much better. It's like being led by the lesser angels of your soul. Dr. Blaine certainly found that to be true. There's something else he also learned—that whenever you include something more in your life, you have to take something or someone out of your life to make room for it. I've had to learn that myself. I think this is what happened to Dr. Blaine. He has had to learn some very painful and hard things. Where he goes from the situation he appears to be locked into, I don't know.

The reason I don't know is that when I started writing this story, I really didn't know what was going happen. It all started as a force or an overflowing of something in me that I had to get out. I just started writing. The story just went and led me and I wrote it down. I had no idea where it was going or how it would end. Actually, it hasn't ended; I've just stopped writing for now. I don't know for how long, but I do know I'd like to revisit Dr. Blaine and see what happens.

I think what I'm going to do is finally turn this last page and take a little time to think about everything that has happened on this journey to Dr. Blaine and myself. A little introspection is probably good for the soul. At least, I should find out where I am right now in life before I take off on another journey. Only by doing that will I really know what direction I'll be going.

Bye for now,
Bruce.

CPSIA information can be obtained
at www.ICGtesting.com
Printed in the USA
LVHW032153020322
712065LV00003B/15/J